TOXICOLOGY

TOXICOLOGY

stories
by

Steve Aylett

FOUR WALLS EIGHT WINDOWS
New York

PUBLISHED IN THE UNITED STATES BY:
Four Walls Eight Windows
39 West 14th Street, room 503
New York, N.Y., 10011

Visit our website at http://www.fourwallseightwindows.com

First printing September 1999.

LIBRARY OF CONGRESS CATALOGING-IN-PUBLICATION DATA
Aylett, Steve, 1967–
    Toxicology : stories / by Steve Aylett.
    p.   cm.
    ISBN 1-56858-131-9
    I. Title.
PR6051.Y57T6   1999
823'.914—dc21   99-33899
                                            CIP

10 9 8 7 6 5 4 3 2 1

Printed in Canada

CONTENTS

"This regime of the surrounding error"
Jacques Rigaut,
Lord Patchogue

"Everything is poison, nothing is poison."
—Paracelsus

"Snake does not bite man; snake bites what man thinks."
—Vinson Brown

"Learning to speak is like learning to shoot."
—Avital Ronell
The Telephone Book

GIGANTIC

Strange aircraft arrived with the sky that morning, moving blood-slow. And Professor Skychum was forced from the limelight at the very instant his ranted warnings became most poignant. "They're already here!"

Skychum had once been so straight you could use him to aim down, an astrophysicist to the heart. No interest in politics—to him Marx and Rand were the same because he went by pant size. Then one afternoon he had a vision which he would not shut up about.

The millennium was the dull rage that year and nutters were in demand to punctuate the mock-emotional retrospectives filling the countdown weeks. The media considered that Skychum fit the bill—in fact they wanted him to wear one.

And the stuff he talked about. There were weaknesses in his presentation, as he insisted that the whole idea occurred to him upon seeing Scrappy Doo's head for the first time. "That dog is a mutant!" he gasped, leaning forward in such a way, and

I

with so precise an appalled squint to the eyes, that he inadver-
tently pierced the constrictive walls of localized space-time. A
flare of interface static and he was seeing the whole deal like a
lava-streamed landscape. He realized he was looking at the psychic holoshape of recent history, sickly and corrosive. Creeping
green flows fed through darkness. These volatile glow trails
hurt with incompletion. They converged upon a cesspit, a
supersick build up of denied guilt. This dumping ground was
of such toxicity it had begun to implode, turning void-black at
its core.

Like a fractal, detail reflected the whole. Skychum saw at once
the entire design and the subatomic data. Zooming in, he
found that a poison line leading from two locations nevertheless flowed from a single event—Pearl Harbor. One source was
the Japanese government, the other was Roosevelt's order to
ignore all warnings of the attack. The sick stream was made up
of 4,575 minced human bodies. In a fast zoom-out, this strand
of history disappeared into the density of surrounding detail,
which in turn resolved into a minor nerve in a spiral lost on the
surface of a larger flow of glowing psychic pollution. A billion
such trickles crept in every tendril of the hyperdense sludge
migration, all rumbling toward this multidimensional landfill of
dismissed abomination. And how he wished that were all.

Future attempts to reproduce his accidental etheric maneu-
ver resulted in the spectacle of this old codger rocking back and
forth with a look of appalled astonishment on his face, an idio-
syncratic and media-friendly image which spliced easily into
MTV along with those colorized clips of the goofing Einstein.
And he had the kind of head propeller hats were invented for.

Skychum went wherever he'd be heard. No reputable journal
would publish his paper *On Your Own Doorstep: Hyperdi-
mensional Placement of Denied Responsibility*. One editor stated

simply: "Anyone who talks about herding behavior's a no-no." Another stopped him in the street and sneered a series of instructions which were inaudible above the midtown traffic, then spat a foaming full-stop at the sidewalk. Chat shows, on the other hand, would play a spooky theremin fugue when he was introduced. First time was an eye-opener. "Fruitcake corner— this guy's got the Seventh Seal gaffa-taped to his ass and claims he'll scare up an apocalypse out of a clear blue sky. Come all the way here from New York City—Dr. Theo Skychum, welcome." Polite applause and already some sniggers. The host was on gar- rulous overload, headed for his end like a belly-laughing Wall of Death rider. How he'd got here was anybody's guess. "Doctor Skychum, you assert that come the millennium, extraterrestrials will monopolize the colonic irrigation industry—how do you support that?"

Amid audience hilarity Skychum stammered that that wasn't his theory at all. The gravity of his demeanor made it all the more of a crack-up. Then the host erupted into a bongo frenzy, hammering away at two toy flying saucers. Skychum was baffled.

He found that some guests were regulars who rolled off the charmed banter with ease.

"Well see here Ray, this life story of yours appears to have been carved from a potato."

"I know, Bill, but that's the way I like it."

"You said you had a little exclusive for us tonight, what's that about?"

"Believe it or not, Bill, I'm an otter."

"Thought so Ray."

It blew by on an ill, hysterical wind and Skychum couldn't get with the program. He'd start in with some lighthearted quip about bug-eyed men and end up bellowing "Idiots!

Discarding your own foundation! Oppression evolves like everything else!"

Even on serious shows he was systematically misunderstood. The current affairs show *The Unpalatable Truth* was expressing hour-long surprise at the existence of anti-government survivalists. This was the eighty-seventh time they'd done this and Skychum's exasperated and finally sobbing repetition of the phrase "even a *child* knows" was interpreted as an attempt to steal everyone's faint thunder. And when his tear-rashed face filled the screen, blurring in and out as he asked "Does the obvious have a reachable bottom?", he was condemned for making a mockery of media debate. A televangelist accused him of "godless snoopery of the upper grief" and, when Skychum told him to simmer down, cursed him with some vague future aggravation. The whole thing was a dismal mess, smeared beyond salvation. Skychum's vision receded as though abashed.

There was no shortage of replacements. One guy insisted the millennium bug meant virtual sex dolls would give users the brush-off for being over a hundred years old and broke. Another claimed he spoke regularly to the ghost of Abe Lincoln. "My communications with this lisping blowhead yield no wisdom at all," he said. "But I'm happy." Then he sneezed like a cropduster, festooning the host with phlegm.

The commentators deemed radical were those going only so far as to question what was being celebrated. Skychum himself found he wanted to walk away. But even he had to admit the turn was a big deal, humanity having survived so long and learned so little—there was a defiant rebelliousness about it that put a scampish grin on everyone's face. For once people were bound with a genuine sense of kick ass accomplishment and self-congratulatory cool. Skychum began at last to wish he was among them. But just as he felt his revelation slipping away, it would seem to him that the mischievous glint in people's eyes redshifted to the power of the Earth itself if viewed from a civilized planet. And his brush with perspective would return with the intensity of a fever dream.

Floating through psychic contamination above a billion converging vitriol channels, toward that massive rumbling cataract of discarded corruption. Drawing near, Skychum had seen that ranged around the cauldroning pit, like steel nuts around a wheel hub, were tiny glinting objects. They were hung perfectly motionless at the rim of the slow vortex. These sentinels gave him the heeby-jeebies, but he zoomed in on the detail. There against the god-high waterfall of volatility. Spaceships.

Ludicrous. There they were.

"If we dealt honestly, maturely with our horrors," he told the purple-haired clown hosting a public access slot, "instead of evading, rejecting and forgetting, the energy of these events would be naturally reabsorbed. But as it is we have treated it as we treat our nuclear waste—where we have dumped it, it is not wanted. The most recent waste will be the first to return."

"Last in, first out eh," said the clown somberly.

"Precisely," said Skychum.

"Well, I wish I could help you," stated the clown with offhand sincerity. "But I'm just a clown."

This is what he was reduced to. Had any of it happened? Was he mad?

A matter of days before the ball dropped in Times Square and Skychum was holed up alone, blinds drawn, bottles empty. He lay on his back, dwarfed by indifference. So much for kicking the hive. The authorities hadn't even bothered to demonize him. It was clear he'd had a florid breakdown, taking it to heart and the public. Could he leave, start a clean life? Everything was strange, undead and dented. He saw again, ghosting across his ceiling, a hundred thousand Guatemalan civilians murdered by US-backed troops. He'd confirmed this afterwards, but how could he have known it before the vision? He only watched CNN. In a strong convulsion of logic, Skychum sat up.

At that moment, the phone rang. A TV guy accusing him of dereliction of banality—laughing that he had a chance to redeem himself and trumpet some bull for the masses. Skychum agreed, too inspired to protest.

It was called *The Crackpot Arena* and it gathered the cream of the foil hat crowd to shoot the rarefied breeze in the hours leading up to the turn. This interlocking perdition of pan-moronic pundits and macabre gripers was helped and hindered by forgotten medication and the pencil-breaking perfectionism of the director. One nutter would be crowned King of the Freaks at the top hour. The criteria were extremity and zero shame at the lectern. Be ridiculed or dubbed the royal target of ridicule—Skychum marvelled at the custom joinery of this conceit. And he was probably in with a chance. In the bizarre stakes, what could be more improbable than justice?

The host's eyes were like raisins and existed to generously blockade his brainlobes. As each guest surfaced from the cracker-barrel he fielded them with a patronizing show of interest.

A man holding a twig spoke of the turn. "All I can reveal," he said, meting out his words like a bait trail, "is that it will be discouraging. And very, very costly."

"For me?" asked the host, and the audience roared.

"For me," said the man, and they were in the aisles.

"Make a habit of monkey antics," declared another guest. "Pleasure employs muscles of enlightenment." Then he led in a screaming chimp, assured everyone its name was Ramone, pushed it down a slide and said "There you go." Skychum told him he was playing a dangerous game.

A sag-eyed old man pronounced his judgment. "The dawn of the beard was the dawn of modern civilization."

"In what way."

"In that time spent growing a beard is time wasted. Now curb this strange melancholy—let us burn our legs with these matches and shout loud."

"I . . . I'm sorry . . . what . . ."

And the codger was dancing a strange jig on the table, cackling from a dry throat.

"One conk on the head and he'll stop dancing," whispered someone behind the cameras.

Another suspect was the ringmaster of the Lobster Circus, who lashed at a wagon-ring of these unresponsive creatures as though at the advancing spawn of the devil. "The time will come," he announced, "when these mothers will be *silent*." And at that he laid the whip into a lobster positioned side-on to him, breaking it in half.

A little girl read a poem:

> behind answers are hoverflies
> properly modest,
> but they will do anything
> for me

One guy made the stone-faced assertion that belching was an actual language. Another displayed a fossilized eightball of mammoth dung and said it was "simply biding its time". Another stated merely that he had within his chest a "flaming heart" and expected this to settle or negate all other concerns.

Then it was straight in with Skychum, known to the host as a heavy-hitter among those who rolled up with their lies at a moment's notice. The host's face was an emulsioned wall as he listened to the older man describe some grandiose reckoning. "Nobody's free until everyone is, right?" was the standard he reached for in reply.

"Until *someone* is."

"Airless Martians still gasping in a town of smashed geodesics," he stated, and gave no clue as to his question. After wringing the laughs out of Skychum's perplexed silence, he continued. "These Martians—what do they have against us?"

"Not Martians—metaversal beings in a hyperspace we are using as a skeleton cupboard. Horror past its sell-by date is dismissed with the claim that a lesson is learned, and the sell-by interval is shortening to minutes."

"I don't understand," said the host with a kind of defiance.

"The media believe in resolution at all costs, and this is only human." Once again Skychum's sepulchral style was doing the trick—there was a lot of sniggering as he scowled like a chef. "Dismissal's easier than learning."

"So you're calling down this evangelical carnage."

"*I'm* not—"

"In simple terms, for the layman"—the eyebrows of irony flipped to such a blur they vanished—"how could all these bodies be floating out in 'hyper' space?"

"Every form which has contained life has its equivalent echo in the super-etheric—if forced back into the physical, these etheric echoes will assume physical shape."

"Woh!" shouted the host, delighted, and the audience exploded with applause—this was exactly the kind of wacko bullshit they'd come to hear. "And why should they arrive at this particular time?"

"They have become synchronized to our culture, those who took on the task—it is appropriate, poetic!"

The audience whooped, flushed with the nut's sincerity.

"The great thing about being ignored is that you can speak the truth with impunity."

"But I call you a fraud, Dr. Skychum. These verbal manipulations cause a hairline agony in the honest man. Expressions of the grave should rival the public? I don't think so. Where's the light and shade?"

Skychum leaned forward, shaking with emotion. "You slur me for one who is bitter and raging at the world. But you mustn't kick a man when he's down, and so I regard the world." Then Ramone the chimp sprang on to his head, shrieking and flailing.

"Dr. Skychum," said the host. "If you're right, *I'm* a monkey."

The ringmaster of the Lobster Circus was declared the winner. The man with the flaming heart died of a coronary and the man with the dung fossil threw it into the audience and stormed off. A throne shaped like the halfshells of a giant nut was set up for the crowning ceremony. Skychum felt light, relieved. He had aquitted himself with honor. He enjoyed the jelly and ice cream feast set up for the contestants backstage. Even the chimp's food-flinging antics made him smile. He approached the winner with goodwill. "Congratulations sir. Those lobsters of yours are a brutal threat to mankind."

The winner looked mournfully up at him. "I love them," he whispered, and was swept away by the makeup crew.

At the moment of the turn, Skychum left the studio building by a side entrance, hands deep in his coatpockets. Under a slouch hat which obscured his sky, he moved off down a narrow street roofed completely by the landscape of a spacecraft's undercarriage.

During the last hour, as dullards were press-ganged onto ferris wheels and true celebrants arrested in amplified streets, hundreds of multidimensional ships had hoved near, denial-allow shields up. Uncloaking, they had appeared in the upper atmosphere like new moons. Now they hove into position over every capital city in the world, impossible to evade. Fifteen miles wide, these immense overshadow machines rumbled across the sky like a coffin lid drawing slowly shut. New York was being blotted out by a floating city whose petalled geometry was only suggested by sections visible above the canyon streets. Grey hieroglyphics on the underside were actually spires, bulkheads and structures of skyscraping size. Its central eye, a mile-wide concavity deep in shadow, settled over uptown as the hovering landscape thundered to a stop and others took up position over London, Beijing, Berlin, Nairobi, Los Angeles, Kabul, Paris, Zurich, Baghdad, Moscow, Tokyo and every other conurbation with cause to be a little edgy. One nestled low over the White House like an inverted cathedral. In the early light they were silent, unchanging fixtures. Solid and subject to the sun.

The President, hair like a dirty iceberg, slapped on a middling smile and talked about caution and opportunity. Everywhere nerves were clouded around with awe and high suspension. Traffic stopped. Fanatics partied. The old man's name was remembered if not his line—a woman held a sign aloft saying I'M A SKY CHUM. Cities waited under dumb, heavy air.

Over the White House, a screeching noise erupted. The central eye of the ship was opening. Striations like silver insect wings cracked, massive steel doors grinding downward.

The same was happening throughout the world, a silver flower opening down over Parliament, Whitehall and the dead Thames; over the Reichstag building, the World Bank, the Beijing Politburo.

The DC saucer eye was open, the bellow of its mechanism echoing away. Onlookers craned to see up inside.

For the space of two heartbeats, everything stopped. Then a tiny tear dropped out of the eye, splashing on the White House roof.

And then another, falling like a light fleck of snow.

These were corpses, these two—human corpses, followed by more in a shower which grew heavier by the moment, some crashing now through the roof, some rolling to land in the drive, bouncing to hit the lawn, bursting to paint the porticoes. And then the eye began gushing.

Everywhere the eyes were gushing. With a strange, continuous, multiphonic squall, the ragged dead rained from the sky.

Sixty-eight forgotten pensioners buried in a mass grave in 1995 were dumped over the Chicago social services. Hundreds of blacks murdered in police cells hit the roof of Scotland Yard. Thousands of slaughtered East Timorese were dumped over the Assembly buildings in Jakarta. Thousands killed in the test bombings at Hiroshima and Nagasaki began raining over the Pentagon. Thousands tortured to death showered Abuja.

Thousands of Sudanese slaves were dumped over Khartoum. The border-dwelling Khmer Rouge found themselves cemented into a mile-high gut slurry of three million Cambodians. Thousands of hill tribesmen were dropped over the Bangladeshi parliament and the World Bank, the latter now swamped irretrievably under corpses of every hue.

Berlin was almost instantly clotted, its streets packed wall to wall with victims. Beijing was swamped with tank fodder and girl babies.

The Pentagon well filled quickly to overflowing, blowing the building outward as surely as a terrorist bomb. Pearl Harbor dupes fell on Tokyo and Washington in equal share. The streets of America flooded with Japanese, Greeks, Koreans, Vietnamese, Cambodians, Indonesians, Dominicans, Libyans, Timorese,

Central Americans and Americans, all beclouded in a pink mist of Dresden blood.

London was a flowing sewer—then the bodies started falling. Parliament splintered like a matchstick model. In the Strand the living ran from a rolling wall of the dead. A king tide of hole-eyed German, Indian, African, Irish and English civilians surged over and against buildings which boomed flat under the pressure. Cars were batted along, flipped and submerged. The Thames flooded its banks, displaced by cadavers.

No longer preserved by denial, they started to sludge. Carpet-bombing gore spattered the suburbs, followed by human slurry tumbling down the streets like lava. Cheap human fallout from pain ignored and war extended for profit. The first wave. So far only sixty years' worth—yet, tilling like bulldozed trash, it spread across the map like red inkblots destined to touch and merge.

Skychum had taken the 8:20 Amtrak north from Grand Central—it had a policy of not stopping for bodies. Grim, he viewed the raining horizon—dust motes in a shaft of light— and presently, quietly, he spoke.

"Many happy returns."

REPEATER

After an hour recording parkbirds I strolled back through town, the mike in my shoulderbag laying down the traffic. Streets like the deeps of a full ashtray. A plainclothes cop trundled up offering drugs. I declined and was arrested. At the kennel the cops were embarrassed and angry when I replayed the proof of my lamblike innocence. As they handed me my jaw on a plate I had an idea. Saw it all red and gold and full of justice. Put it at the front of a piece of Debussy and let the music carry it forward, filling it out. A notion and a half. Have to ask the old soldier.

The beating was over and I hadn't noticed. Cops regarding me with stall-cod eyes. Time to get up—but don't do it again.

Back on the street feeling four snapped ribs—I've had worse and laughed with the correct medication. It was partly my fault for taking that route. The area was famous for the cops' planting of drugs and users had begun flocking there in the hope of being able to keep some in exchange for violence. But I wondered what Dogger would say.

The old soldier lived in a shed made of biscuit and was never without his dog Fire, the calling of whose name caused alarm and mayhem. Dogger had dodged so many bad laws his spine had corkscrewed. In classic style he had swallowed media promises of a better life and then overstepped the boundary of etiquette by actually trying to secure one. He was like Fagin without the charm and carried lemons in his coat as a tear gas precaution. He was so real his toaster ran on diesel. As I descended the railway embankment I heard him yelling in the hut. "The chains of your repression are as familiar to you as the teeth in your head. Born to it you were."

"Hello Dogger," I said cautiously, entering—he was alone. I told him about the cops' theft of my equipment.

"There's no limit to what a dying system will demand of you, Hypnojerry," he laughed, showing braces like a knuckleduster. "Only a narrow land could end at one stroke the right to sound and the right to silence." He was referring to a brace of laws which curtailed the activities of those with an aptitude for reflection and enjoyment. "For fear of copycat outbreaks of happiness and laughter. Not that the deeper implications matter to a public soundproofed by indifference. Sad as a galleon in a bottle."

His hands flew over the eight-track sound desk. He was messing with the sound of a prefab saying "nothing you need fear"—it was reversed, accelerated, cracked like a whip. "They did the same to me—tried to send me to clench for heseltine possession." This was a laugh as cocaine would have slowed Dogger's thoughts to a constabulary crawl. He had an eight-track mind. "It's genius envy, Jell, pure and sour. I felt pity for the bastards so as not to get too angry. Injustice rings down through history to a deserted callbox. Let stress get into your tripes you'll end up in surgery under a blithe knife. Watch this."

And he played the word "fear" while pointing to a screen where the sound was rendered as a geometrical netshape which bulbed like a soapbubble. He tapped at a keyboard which froze the shape, then flipped it inside-out like a mitten. "Now let's play this shape as a noise," he said, and pressed return. The system emitted the worst fart I'd ever heard.

Dogger explained that he had found a way to disclose the inner nature of a recorded verbal statement. Some remarks produced the zenlike sound of a gong. Others—particularly those of the young—the howl of a desert wind. Politicians from both dum and dee almost always created flatulence.

It was the latest in a long course of experimentation. Dogger had discovered birdsong slowed down was whalenoise and whalenoise speeded up was birdsong. He found that Nixon's resignation speech reversed was an invocation to the Devil in exquisitely pronounced Lithuanian. When he heard about the rave laws outlawing repetitive beats he examined the issue in fly-leg detail. Rhythm requires an alternation between sound and silence, or one sound and another. Dogger had considered whether the legislation could apply to repetitive injustice and bullshit but these activities were so constant as to be a seamless, mundane hum. Only regular interruptions of this mundanity could set up a beat. That was why raves were against the law— so that the unjust and dishonest would not be seen to be part of an illegal process. "It's all in the game, Hypnojerry. Mischief distinguishes man from the other animals—that and the opposable thumb."

A train shrieked past and Fire woke up, raising his ears and eyebrows.

The next evening we retrieved my gear with the help of Antifrog. We figured since two wrongs don't make a right our act would not stand out against the general corruption.

Antifrog was a gay black youth with a strong Irish accent and herbal trousers. When this montage of minorities swanned into the kennel the cops couldn't believe their luck and set about his punishment. Truncheons leapt like salmon as he tried to report a theft. Dogger and I slipped past before the party was dampened by blood and boredom.

Since the passing of the new laws so much sound equipment had been seized we had learned that the safest thing to do was break into the cop confiscation store and dump our stuff there without a tag. Other than drugs they never touched a thing. But with the party approaching we'd need the gear and for once we had a legitimate reason for entry—my recording rig. Dogger kept up a running commentary as he worked the bolt cutters—he'd speak till the bitter, amp-smashing end. "Almost gave up on your generation, Jell. Tunnel vision without a flashlight. A passionless blank. Then by god the color started seeping out of the walls. Back from the dead—and me too. Should have seen me in the eighties, boy—so out of it I had sideburns on someone else's face. Then one day I strode toward the horizon and was damn near garrotted by a rainbow."

We were into the storeroom—I found my gear and knew this was the only way I could have retrieved it. The truth is easiest to disprove—its defenses are down.

Dogger meanwhile was flashing a Mysteron beam over amplifier stacks—the stuff of villainy. "Jell, disorder's an offense with no mappable contours and the ideal fog for all occasions. Laws have gone by like motes on the film of my eye and with as much effect—but disorder? By god it's a beauty."

"We're in a hurry-up," I reminded him.

But Dogger had a philosophy you could stand a spoon in— he took a book from a shelf, blowing at the dust and frowning.

"*After London*. Damn fine book—you can keep your triffids. Jefferies got there first, with a flood. Well written too."

"Most books are so well written they barely have any effect on the reader's senses," I told him urgently. "Let's conclude this procedure and get out."

"With a bang or a whimper though Jell, how'd you picture it ending? The world, I mean?" We lifted the stack amp between us and started off. "Here's how I see it," Dogger grunted through his exertions. "Denial. Vacuum competes with vacuum. Laws outlaw the harmless to make the effective inconceivable. Scholarly incomprehension. No questions asked. Banality given the terms and prestige of science. Ignorance worn like a heraldic crest. Mediocrity loudly rewarded. Misery by installments. Hypocrisy too extreme to process. Maintenance of a feeble public imagination. Lavish access to useless data. Fashion as misdirection. Social meltdown in a cascade pattern, consumed by a drought of significance. Drabness as ordered as the grey cells of a deserted waspnest."

"It's a thought."

On the way out we were approached by someone as featureless as a figure in a crash procedure diagram. It asked who we were and we pretended to be cops by saying we didn't know.

A few days later we visited Antifrog in hospital. The beating had been worse than we expected but he wished us well through a broken mouth. We taped the irregular bleep of his coronary monitor and set off for the country. A convoy of cars processioned through darkness toward a repeated thumping which could have been the heartbeat of the land itself. By degrees it became audible as Ravel's *Bolero*, played across a fallow field stretching so far it seemed not to end. Acres of grass were blown to italics. Fire leapt from the van and started across the field, eager for fun.

By midnight the field was a sea of ethnic trousers and Evian bottles. I remember weird strobe images of Dogger looking as spooky as a pickled alien. Lasers of jade and red gold were fanning and dipping as Antifrog's heartrate formed the grid for a soundscape sampled from the net and forced through a 50,000 watt sound system. In the crowd it was hard to tell where one smile ended and another began. Without lying there was nothing bad to be said about it. The press would have a field day.

Dogger and I had wired ourselves and some others with cop-style bodymikes which relayed crowdnoise through an oscillating sampler. Dogger disappeared but I heard him talking again, taking full advantage of the mike—rantbites were firing off and jarring with the ambience. "Cancering anxiety. Sneering at tradition. A government openly at war with its people. Why be covert in the last ditch?" I waded through the scene to strangle him—no polemics, Dogger, not *now*.

I saw blurlights playing over a marquee wall and wondered how a set of old pub strobes had got in here. A repetitive siren effect was cranked up in the mix—*this sound is illegal*, I thought vaguely, and passing outside found it was caused by countless police cars surrounding the area. Blue lights strobed in the night.

The cops stood expecting our amusement to be paralyzed in deference. Many had confused their profession with full human identity. I thought a few had guns, and asked someone why.

"To assure us that nice people carry guns too."

One cop was yelling inaudibly through a megaphone. I learned later that this official warning to leave was a mere formality, but as the cop put the hailer aside and signalled the others to move in, a loop of his statement volleyed from the speakerstacks. Most of the ravers took it as a joke but a thousand wandered out and the cops, finding they had lost the element of surprise, panicked.

Looking back I can see all the components of hell were assembled. The cops terrified the crowd in an ironic and postmodern attempt to provoke order. A few less educated ravers didn't get the reference and became angry. These signals were elaborately ignored and the order to move on repeated. Again someone's mike picked up the message and rendered it audible, increasing the crowd outside the main tent. The cops said that failure to comply would be considered an act of aggression. Dizzy with the notion that a thing could be considered something it wasn't, the crowd yelled back that cop helmets would be considered anchovies and that the cops themselves were chimps in cashmere. There was a cold explosion.

Add velocity to ignorance and you get a police car. One sped into the crowd and screeched to a halt as a girl twisted through the air and landed in a heap. A new sound spat out of the speakers—a crack and then a squelch, like someone treading on a snail. Near the cop ranks someone's head had been rolled over—grey brain tangled with grey hair. It was Dogger.

Amid the sequencers and scenes of riot several wired subjects were beaten repeatedly, each blow being re-broadcast from the rave stacks. A mile away, plaster ducks fell from cottage walls as the sound of a skull being struck repeatedly echoed through the early hours. The regular succession of blows made looping redundant. The rhythm of three different beatings merged and intersected like a multitracking beatbox, the occasional bonesnap an added punctuation. Rather than look vigilantly the other way, senior officers drove the mayhem. Blood dark as spilled petrol flared pillar-box red in the streak of torchbeams.

Shots were followed by screams. Windscreens spiderwebbed, smoke drifted and the volume increased as shadowy figures became meaningless smudges of chaotic movement.

A cold sun rose over the ghost of a good time. A few survivors wandered dazed. Picking through a dawn of Chaplin grey I wished Dogger was alive or wrong. But he was neither and his passing was a deadbolt on any objective reflection. As far as I was concerned there had once been giants in the earth and now there was only plastic. Truth withered on the vine as the raid was declared a victory for common sense. Four deaths not including Dogger, who didn't count because he was old, and twelve others who didn't count because they weren't cops either. It was clarified that repetitive beating of a live skull in the course of police duty was legal but that acoustic amplification of the sound was not. The rave organizers, who had hired the land, decided to save money by trespassing for the next event.

I had Fire to look after. This charge looked to me in expectation of something I couldn't guess. Finally he decided I wasn't Dogger and wandered off. My generation lacked some essential element—I only hoped this made us unpredictable.

The authorities had taken action hoping some miracle would prevent an equal and opposite reaction, but no miracle materialized. Youth retaliation was swift and violent though sad beyond its years. Dogger had called us a dull bruise pounded over and over. A sleepy generation with the rave scene acting as a giant alarm. And he never would listen when I told him the weariness was understandable, for a brood overseen by those who make the same mistake and act surprised at the same result again and again and again and again and again and again and again.

JAWBREAKER

☼

Terry Tantamount lived like a kitten struggling up stairs. He never had the faintest idea of the right thing to say in any given situation. And it seemed there was a very specific right and wrong to this.

"Have I put on weight?"

"Yeah, thank god."

At a dinner party once he held two lobsters facing each other and puppetted a conversation—even here he didn't parp the appropriate exchange. People flinched with embarrassment. Sometimes he saw them trying to cover for him but mostly he just saw disappointment, scorn, anger—even disgust.

"Don't tell me you've been asleep all this time."

"Okay."

Sometimes the desired answer was clued in the question but it seemed such an absurd shell game—did people think so little of themselves they wanted to be lied to?

"Hey babe, if I didn't know better I'd say you were jealous."

"Sure I am, honey."

In childhood these misfires had the immediacy of a poptart burn but as time lagged it became a dull bruise pummelled over and over. He learned that "How are you?" wasn't a question, and other basics. But he didn't understand it and could no more than dip his beak. How to proceed? Grow a pelt of dignity? Feign indifference? It was torment without thunder.

"Republican or Democrat?"

"Are those my options?"

Terry's fanciful notions of honesty and sense made him as popular as a burning tire. When questioned directly about their sources, people displayed such absolute resolve to dodge the issue, Terry usually took pity and relented. If backed into a corner they became hostile or at the very least emphatically dishonest prior to hasty retreat. It seemed they were doing yeoman's work in someone else's notions.

"Guess what I've got."

"A deadly hidden agenda?"

At first he thought his girlfriend Yanda could teach him the cues in this baggy pants farce. But she seemed evasive, even ashamed. "Nobody asks questions like that," she said. But Terry existed. He had no choice but to assume she didn't mean it. That way lay madness. Every dawn he said a plain noble prayer for communication.

"What about them Yankees?"

"Yeah, what about 'em?"

But facts are found where temptation is brightest. Terry had noticed Yanda always got a lot of mail—one package minimum. The one time she didn't, she seemed at a loss. She even yelled at him in the middle of a discussion, "What am I meant to say to that?" It was the only time she didn't know her own dialogue.

The idea entered his head like a fox bellying under a fence. When Yanda was out a couple days later, he searched the house. Under the bed was a postal packet containing a thin script. Lead treasure.

"Have I put on weight?"

"Of course not."

"Don't tell me you've been asleep all this time."

"Of course not."

"Hey babe, if I didn't know better I'd say you were jealous."

"Of course not."

"Republican or Democrat?"

"Democrat."

"Guess what I've got."

"Oh great—I love that game."

"What about them Yankees?"

"Yeah, fourth and ten, ball on their thirty yard line with only forty seconds to go."

The script included every correct response for the day's exchanges between Yanda and himself. That evening he batted them back at Yanda and her face lit up. At first Terry loved seeing her believe this was him, but quickly became disgusted by her delight. Didn't she value the genuine article at all? And this stuff was so drab, so uninspired. It took an effort for him not to add splashes of color. But he knew that upset people.

He traced the mail source to a complex in the city. He'd hoped this at least would be interesting—a Mount Weather-style bunker or Pinay cabal. But it was an unmanned factory emitting no light. The same beige streams of dialogue were continually recycled under grey stacks, the blind produce of identical codes, bound and labelled for delivery. There was neither sentience nor malevolence in this automation. Energy was neither created nor destroyed in writ so poor.

Examining the records, Terry learned that his own scripts were being delivered in error to a *Telly* Tantamount right in his town. He dropped by the guy's house and was greeted at the door by a crazed, seething wreck, a jumpy cadaver with deodorant balls for eyes. "Told ya I don't want any!" shrieked the guy, terrified. Terry's heart went out to him.

"Telly? I know what you've been going through. Nothing connects? You've been getting scripts meant for me, man. Admin goof."

The man stared. "I . . . I don't know what to say." And Terry saw relief flood him, pushing tears from his face.

Reading over some of the old scripts the man had given him, Terry ambled home. He was supposed to have said this stuff? It was insipid—false and impoverished. No wonder people were ashamed to admit they accepted it above their own spirit. He'd long suspected that if he ever discovered the nature of the game he would find it too dumb and unrewarding to play anyway. To be so hen-hearted? To live his life as stock footage? To guard forever against divergence into originality? To what end? And what would be left to him? By comparison his life of stress and concern thus far seemed a funky adventure.

And wasn't he the lucky one. He felt an easy freedom, his limbs hanging light in his joints, while at the same time his heart bled with compassion for the folk he passed. Here he'd been suffering and all these were here too, without the born spark even to fight or tell it.

"Was it busy out?"

"Yanda," he said, sitting down heavily and dropping the scripts aside. "Listen. I'm not really in any hurry to be illuminated. Heaven doesn't tolerate cunning or wit. This grub in the head's an inconvenience, I realize that, and I should probably say I'm sorry, though that's just a guess on my part. But I want you to know. Despite your sentences being a barricade to truth. Despite your approval existing only for trifles. Despite your gargantuan efforts to bury yourself, deny your mind and cremate your courage. Despite your attempt to remove all distinguishing marks—I see you. You're an angel, babe. Mad, soft round the edges, scared, and trying your damnedest with what you have. I love you down to the deepest atom. What do you say to that?"

TUSK

After a pert little heist one day Easy Fortezza felt unaccountably reluctant to remove his mask. It was the amiably layered face of an elephant. He wasn't even meant to participate in such heists, let alone become transmogrified into a tusken behemoth during the procedure. Because he was a favorite nephew of Eddie Thermidor the gang boss, everyone indulged him. But when after a whole week he was still wearing the bonce, some of the house hoods had a sit-down about it. "So he's got a attitude problem," shrugged Larry Crocus, cracking his knuckles.

"Attitude," grunted Moray.

"Maybe it's a phase," said Sam "Sam" Bleaker.

"Phase," grunted Moray.

"You guys'll be the death o' me," laughed Barry Nosedive.

"Death," grunted Moray.

"I mean it's not like he's done any harm," Nosedive continued. "Maybe he's evolving under the pressure."

"He poses the threat of a good example," hissed Shiv, examining his knife.

"Sure. We'll get a reputation."

"Death," grunted Moray.

"We can't waste Fortezza," stated Nosedive. "He's good—irreplaceable."

"He appears to have been effortlessly replaced by an elephant," muttered Mr. Flak without inflection. He was a man who did not have to raise his voice as he cared little whether anyone heard him—and no one ever did.

"This droopy mammal," hissed Shiv, "cow-eyed and inscrutable, will kill us all."

"The boss don't even know Easy goes out on them installation pieces," added Bleaker. "He finds out about this the lot of us'll be found on an empty lot with our future round our ankles."

"And our ears stuffed with miniveggies," hissed Shiv.

"Let me talk to the boy," muttered Mr. Flak. "He trusts me."

No one heard the older guy.

"Death," grunted Moray.

Mr. Flak visited Easy's apartment for a friendly chat on the matter of the boys' decision to send him to the ivory yard. As he waited for Easy to show, the boys planted a bomb on each corner of the building in a deliberate deviation from mob intervention method. Only one went off, obliterating Mr. Flak and the apartment, and the feds suppressed knowledge of the others thinking it was another covert job gone sloppy. Thermidor clocked the mob style but concluded it was a rival gang—maybe Betty getting above her strata. Considering Easy and Mr. Flak were both dead of dispersion, he declared gang war.

Easy meanwhile went on the skitter deep underground in Beerlight City, too tired and tangled to retaliate. Had he offended, or been offended against? At what point had he diverged into this dumb fugitive routine? He knew that among those who suspected his survival he was banished. He wept tears thick as glue.

But he finally found he wasn't alone regarding the masks. There was even a support group for crooks in just his situation. One night he was listening to one of his brother sufferers address the group. "My name's Josh," the brother was saying. "And I've been wearing Newt Gingrich's face for . . . three years now. Unlike many of you, I can never feel pride. But I'm resolved to live with the abuse, the scorn, the hatred—and live life as best I can. That's all I have to say." There was applause as Josh sat down. Easy later heard that a plastic surgeon had altered the mask to Boris Karloff by shortening the forehead.

But that evening as Josh sat down, Easy beheld a pale horse sitting to his right—the sleekest creature he'd ever seen. After the meeting she approached him. "You don't need this any more than I do, tusker."

"So why you here?"

"Ill will hunting. I'm Lady Miss V. Short for Voltaire—I run the Fist of Irony under Valentine Street. The meek are welcome to the earth, Easy." The pony girl led him across town and down a stairwell to a basement entrance. She pointed out a light meter over the door to measure PVC gleam intensity and took him in.

The Fist of Irony illuminated all the ghostly bones of the heart. Rather than just biting the bullet, these people strapped on a feedbag. Among the laser-sprayed crowd were Chewy Endeavor, a skeleton glossed with wetlook leather, Annie Drawback, who'd disconnected her headskin to make it a draw-off woman hood, Ted Gloot, a man trapped in a cop's body, and hundreds more who, sick of being stared at in drab America, had resolved to legitimize the stares. Someone had grown a beard consisting entirely of facial muscle. Others had directly stained their skulls with a likeness of their own face so as to retain personality in the grave. A black guy had had himself tattooed all over with the US flag so that police assault might result in prosecution. Couples into acting out alien abductions found common cause with the enema crowd. Buddha Gore had replaced his eyes with wadded-up memos and stuffy apologia. Ariel Hi-Blow was such an invert he stuck himself to the ceiling and put a mirror on the floor. "Molecular solvent," he laughed, and Easy looked up, startled. "I can see up your pants."

FMJ the gunhead wore a bullet suit and had had Lady Miss construct a giant Charter Arms .44 Special to his precise specifications. "Tonight's the night," he said.

"Go girl," yelled Ariel from the ceiling.

The Caere Twins were in the corner with a guy in a void coat—one pushed an arm in up to the elbow and brought it out dripping with ectoplasm. The man extruded an etheric valve and slathered them in blown ghost—the entire corner bulbed into a pullulating chrysalis, sickly with spinelight. Peering at the indistinct forms which wrestled within the calyx, Easy was hustled on past a series of doors. "Tug of War Room— don't go in there. Hillary Room—private party. Mattel Room—slaves. Firing range—need a license. And here's my chamber." Lady led him into a stable. "America kisses with its mouth closed, Easy. Want to try something?" She placed a bit between her teeth, separating her jaws, and buckled the strap behind her head.

"We can't do this, Lady," stammered Easy. "It's unnatural— we're different species."

Lady shrugged off her clothes and knelt over, gleaming

white. Easy felt like an airbag was being deployed in his skull. An explosion sounded over the building as FMJ reached for the sky.

Two whole years passed. Easy became part-owner of the club. Moving in a different world, he kept clear of the mob. For a crook to become attached to his disguise was an offense without duplicity. It was rejection—growth, even. Like others at the Fist, he'd given up trying to deny the worth of worship.

Holdup masks never went out of fashion—one afternoon Larry Crocus, Moray, Shiv, Bleaker and Barry Nosedive were due to perform a heist behind the faces of a regular menagerie. The job had reached the vault when Shiv, who had selected the face of a walrus, raised a gun at the others. "Cut it out, Shiv," they laughed nervously.

With a rubbery flourish, he drew off the walrus mask to reveal that of an elephant.

"Fortezza!" gasped Larry Crocus.

"That's right," said Easy. "Character don't take orders."

Nosedive pushed forward, the ears of his dog mask flapping. "Hey we gave you the cod eye!"

"I have different information."

Crocus, who wore the face of a pig, gestured to Easy with his snubgun. "Where's the face we shut."

"This is who I am." He drew a bead on Crocus. "And these beans want planting."

"Four guns to one, Dumbo," honked Moray from behind a cat face.

At that moment, Sam "Sam" Bleaker tore off his horse mask to reveal that of a horse.

"Who the hell are you?" shouted Crocus as the pale horse aimed her gun. "What you do with Bleaker and Shiv?"

"You bore me," said Lady.

"Tied up in a closet at the gang fort," said Easy. "They didn't come along on the bomb run, after all."

"So it's about the old man. We don't got any gripe with you Easy but I'll put you on a keyboard if I have to."

"I don't bluff empty armor, guys. Lemme ask you, is crime what happens when you miss the target, or hit it? I put glue in your masks."

The three mobsters dropped their guns and began scrabbling at their heads as Easy and Lady Miss backed out of the vault. It was Ariel Hi-Blow's molecular glue. A scream tore out as a face came away with a fake.

An elephant never forgets.

THE WAFFLE CODE

Inside every fat man is a thin man trying to get out—inside that thin man is an even thinner man, and so on. The final stage is like a fiber strand from a dead branch. Knowing this, Chief Henry Blince never started down that road. His belly was the near side of an unexplored gas planet. He was gargling with potato salad when Benny the Trooper radioed in, calling him to warm his hands at a crime scene on Galas Street.

"Whatta we got Benny?" he rumbled, entering the premises.

"One cord wonder, Chief."

"Hanging?"

"And then some."

"Cocktail homicide?" Blince asked, lumbering down the hallway after Benny. "What else?"

"Head start."

"Shot in the temple eh."

"Kitchen, Chief. Poison in his pump too, say forensics. Ain't been dead long—body's still smoking."

The pulse loser hung by the neck from a light fitting, riddled with 9mm caliber airholes. "What kinda gun was used? Like it matters."

"Steyr sub pistol, Chief."

"That's a tantrum gun. When you say 'sub' you've said it all, eh? Ballistics took it?"

"No Chief, it's here." Benny gestured to a gun on a tripod, a length of string tied to the trigger, five feet from the body. Another shorter piece of string hung from the victim's ear. "Seven rounds left in a fifteen mag. Eye-bolt high on the wall there—reckon he pulleyed the string so the flaw went off when he dropped—string broke but by then he'd got half a set."

"Now hold your horses, Benny," said the Chief, lighting a Hindenberg. "Don't you recognize this meat puppet? This here's Fraph Cargill. Fraph had many faults but being dead was never one of 'em."

"Sure, you liked him for that candy factory break-in and he mouthed all off." A conspiracy nut famous for triangulating sacred angles off the roof of Snoopy's kennel, Fraph had blamed Blince for the break-in, whining of persecution. Witnesses claimed to have seen Blince at the scene but the figure had been officially declared a weather balloon. "Still, the boys in forensics see this here baby as open and shut."

"The boys in forensics are faggots. Remember the Hurley Murder? We walk onto the crime scene to find 'em lyin' down makin' gore angels? I suspect for a fact that this is homicide. Now let's take a wry look at the evidence the forensics boys saw fit to ignore. The raisin on the counter, for light starters."

"Cut it out, Chief—you're killin' me."

Blince gave Benny a level, slack-faced gaze. "Well, looky here. The trooper boy doubts my sincerity. Well let's put it to the test, shall we. You recall that auto-erotic hangin' a couple years back? Best orange I ever tasted. Well the coroner said the stiff had taken minutes to die—maybe Fraph here tried leavin' a clue to the killer's identity."

"Chief, I—"

"Don't be interruptin' me, Benny, or I'll bust your ass. And that means you won't be able to . . . ? Won't be able to . . . ?"

"Siddown?"

"On the goddamn money. Now put this raisin in water so it turns back into a grape—there may be a message scrawled on it."

In a while Benny pitched up with a glass of water in which a dark grape was rolling. "Nothing Chief."

"Am I nuts or is the water discolored Benny?"

"Both."

"So the message could have been washed away by you droppin' it in your water—nice move, trooper boy."

"You crack me up Chief, you really do."

"Eh?" Blince paused to eat the grape and wash it down with the water. "This guy scrawls the killer's name on the nearest and dearest surface and you wipe it clean like a guilty slate. All we know now is it's a real short name."

"I been tryin' to tell ya, Chief, he left a ditch note on the table here, under a waffle iron."

Benny handed him a sheet of paper on which were penned the words "Blince rejects reason, torments hounds and ducks blame. Will my end help?"

"Waffle iron eh? This one here?"

"Handwriting checks out, Chief."

"I don't doubt it, Benny. Smart. Real smart."

"What yuh gettin' at?"

"Cargill was a conspiracy nut, right? The type to find messages in the Bill o' Rights? There's twelve words in this so-called ditch note, Benny. Same number as the holes in the grid o' this waffle iron. Arrange the words in the same pattern as that grid—four rows o' three words. He left a message alright."

"I don't get it, Chief."

"Well, Benny—if that is your real name—take a swatch at the body here." He gestured over his shoulder with the cigar. "Eight—count them—eight bullets, all told. Told if you've ears to hear. This man used his own death wounds as a cipher, trooper boy."

"That takes tough chewing, Chief," said Benny with a furrowed brow and a bright smirk.

"Does it? Picture the scene, Benny. A man forced at gunpoint to write his own suicide note and to assign some spurious guilt to me. He pitches the argument that if he's set to die for it, it might as well be done right, in his own style so as not to arouse suspicion. The killer falls for it. And so Mr. Personality chooses this form of words, placing the waffle iron on it supposedly as a paperweight. Then the killer strings him up, poisons him, and shoots him with the TMP. I know what you're gonna say, Benny—why'd he keep on firing the gun, waitin' to hear if it'd play a different note? No. Fraph taunted him, calling him all the names he could pronounce, baiting him into emptying half a clip and leaving the body as we view it today, lame red herrings and all."

"You can't know that, Chief."

"I can know whatever I like, trooper boy." Blince gestured at the victim's purple face. "Cargill understood it. And speakin' o' red herrings, Benny, do fish got eyelids? I mean you'd figure with the driftin' detritus and all, they'd wanna blink maybe eighty times a minute. Or sleep, for god's sake."

"I heard sharks fall to the seafloor if they stop movin', Chief.

Heart stops on a dime. No independent cardiac action. No swim bladder."

"And no eyelids. Well I guess you oughta count your blessings, trooper boy."

Blince sat down at the small table, flipped the ditch note and took up a pencil, writing it out in a three-by-four grid pattern. "Pull up a chair, Benny—we got a puzzle to solve. What was Fraph Cargill really tryin' to tell the world?"

"You just slay me, Chief," chuckled Benny, shaking his head as he honked a chair across and sat down.

"Eight rounds fired, seven unfired, eight divided by seven and rounded down a little is one. Word one, word seven, word eight. 'Blince ducks blame.' That's just a trial run, let's get into this for real now. That was three numbers. Eight rounds—eight divided into three numbers, well how about one, five, two. 'Blince hounds rejects.' No, no. Eight and seven times three, minus eight and divide into three's maybe twelve, ten, seven, eight, one—'Help my ducks—blame Blince.' Just warmin' up here, Benny. Eight plus seven is fifteen which is three numbers there, so minus three's twelve—one, four and seven is 'Blince torments ducks.' God almighty—throw me a bone here, trooper boy."

"My ducks blame Blince."

"Help end my torments. Blame Blince."

"Blince will end reason."

"Blince will blame my ducks."

"Blince torments my hounds."

"Will Blince help rejects?"

"Will Blince duck blame?"

"Blince hounds ducks."

"Will my torments end? Help! Blame Blince!"

"My end. Reason? Blince."

"End my Blince torments."

"Blame Blince and my ducks will help."

"This guy's sure got a thing about his ducks, Chief."

"It's becoming clear to me Fraph got in way over his head with this secret message gambit. Seen the kinda thing before— a man tries goin' too smart and overflows the system. Ironic as a silenced Jericho ain't it? Remember when old Leon Wardial was placid and content to break and enter dressed as a nun and so forth? Then he catches ideas, launches that balloon, says he's happier than he's ever been. Like he's too good for the street." Leon Wardial's armed airship the *Hollow Oak* circled the globe just slower than the planetary spin so that it appeared to be flying backward through the sky. On its stern, first to emerge over the horizon, was an immense gaseous arse. One day a pig went berserk in the engine room, damaging equipment and reducing propulsion by five percent. As a result onlookers around the world saw a single bob and descent of the gargan- tuan butt at the vanishing point. "Never a dull moment though, I'll give him that."

"So whatta we do with the message, Chief?"

"Well, Benny, the first steadying influence Fraph'll have in his life is when we cut him down—he's bitten off way more'n he can chew here. He wanted martyrdom he'll get it anyhow. Every victim is loved after some initial time, they'll even lami- nate your ass. We need to start out by deciding what it was he meant to say. Then you know how Wardial says he built that balloon by reverse-engineerin' an alien gag that crashed and burned on open mike night in the Reaction Bar? We gotta use the same kinda modus operandi. God forbid that a person starts resistin' change. Especially in death, eh Benny? Now let's take a look here. 'My will: help Blince end reason. Torments?

Rejects? Blame hounds and ducks.' There. That'll do. Twelve words, minus the two of us is ten. Minus Fraph is nine. Twelve words is twelve. One victim is one. One off twelve takes care of eleven. The three of us is three. See how this is workin', Benny? Eight rounds fired divided by us is four. The two of us is two. Eight rounds is eight. Us plus him plus us is five. Plus him is six. Seven rounds unfired is seven. We've cracked it."

"I guess. But I still reckon homicide'll be tough to swallow, Chief."

"What a man can't swallow defines him, trooper boy. Make me believe my duty's superfluous and *that's* homicide. The law starts in brass and lives in my ass like a load. What is it with you? Shut the truth in with a goat and block your ears—you know the drill."

"Hey wait a minute, Chief—I just realized I got it ass backward. It was seven rounds fired and eight left, not the other way."

"Just like that eh. Well ain't that dandy. Thanks, trooper boy—thanks for the help. What, I gotta do everythin' myself? Lemme see, here." Blince stood and lumbered to the Steyr. Ignoring the meaning of his act, he shunted the safety to the right for single shot. Then he lined up on the body, corner-biting his cigar.

"This is the last favor I do for you, Cargill."

A fresh shot set the corpse spinning.

IF ARMSTRONG WAS INTERESTING

If Armstrong was interesting he'd take the initiative on stepdown. He'd emerge from the moon capsule wearing Mickey Mouse ears. He'd confess to a major felony. He'd land lightly and trill "Not bad for a girl." He'd shout "Jeez Louise I could use a bacon sandwich" or "Praise be to Satan" or "More land to pillage and despoil" or "This is nowhere" or "Lock up your daughters" or "Who farted?" or "I've never been so bored" or "I've never been so hard" or "Looky here — a million strawberries" or "Kill the white man" or "I was brought here against my will" or "I can't live a lie anymore — I'm gay."

If Armstrong was interesting he'd phonetically blur his assigned lines — "That's one small pecker, man — one tired leaker, and mine." He'd slam from the capsule roaring drunk. He'd skip across the sands like a fairy. He'd pretend to meet aliens and narrate false thrills amid nonexistent domes of tessellated gold. He'd plant the Chilean flag. He'd wheely and wreck that crappy car. He'd claim the whole thing was a movie

set. He'd speak in seamless, uneditable profanity. He'd laugh
without interruption. He'd rant bitterly against his mother.
He'd scream at a pitch which blew the headphones off NASA
control. He'd say everything in a thick French accent. He'd yell
that his facemask was filling with snot and abruptly terminate
transmission. He'd moan "Even here there's pigeons." He'd ask
"If I'm the first man to walk here, who set up the camera to
film it?" He'd pretend transmission was breaking into enigmatic
fragments. He'd say "demonic" and "pants" and "fantastic" and
"farewell." He'd neigh and say "Woah, there." He'd childishly
mimic everything Houston said. He'd curse the Earth and
claim the moon's supremacy. He'd moon and decompress,
exploding.

If Armstrong was interesting he'd emerge from the capsule
riding Buzz Aldrin piggyback with a horsewhip. He'd ruthlessly
probe Buzz's sexuality. He'd slap a squid over Buzz's visor,
blinding him. He'd get him in an awkward headlock. He'd try
repeatedly to run him down with the buggy, mouthing laughter in the vacuum. He'd snap a thousand contrary orders,
dancing sarcastically to his own contradictions. He'd ask once
every minute on the return trip "Are we there yet?" He'd
emerge from the space toilet sweating, pupils constricted, and
threaten the copilots with a blender. He'd draw them into his
madness so that after splashdown they'd prance out of the
rescue vehicle giggling and pushing each other into the bushes.

If Armstrong was interesting he'd attend a press conference
wearing a hat made of a human pelvis fringed with the
shrunken ears of his victims. He'd say the whole trip was a
waste of time. He'd complain that his critical judgment had
"turned to jelly." He'd describe his own eyelashes as "a delight,"
speaking at first in a stage whisper, then screaming into the

mike and blowing eardrums like popcorn. He'd fall at every hurdle. He'd purse his lips to his fist and trumpet *The Red Flag*. He'd guffaw. He'd announce "I crave the company of morticians. I love everything about them. You'll be glad to hear I live in a ghastly dreamworld. And you can't stop me."

If Armstrong was interesting he'd sell baby crocs on TV for "crazy prices." He'd crash into people's front rooms in the cab of a beaked ironclad Russian locomotive. He'd work as the actor inside the rigid costume of Gamera, the giant turtle which flies by means of a nuclear arse. He'd fashion underwear for ungrateful, unresponsive bugs. He'd build a papier mâché demon with beautiful legs. He'd thrash miniveggies from the banquet table. He'd toss frogs from a speeding car. He'd dropkick a master chef. He'd promise the warden he'd see him in hell. He'd say urbanely "Put it on his bill over there—him with the dead eyes." He'd prong his own nose with an ancient eel fork. He'd flaunt his head, god's gift to snipers. He'd grimace like a tailor. He'd put a flea in the deity's ear by capering like a chimp. He'd evince groggy surprise. He'd impregnate his lunch. He'd pistol-whip a troll. He'd say "We are sisters in tennis." He'd enter a casino with a shovel. He'd burn formality through the night. He'd visit gas upon clowns. He'd become a hive of teeth. He'd leak genes coveted by the scrabbling poor. He'd don the bell-sleeves of a magus and rain down mellow blessings upon his people. He'd go as loose as a flower. He'd smile wan and leave. He'd grow soft pink fur and stink of diesel. He'd say "Just think of it. Octopi for everyone. Yellow conclusions of a thousand years. Am I dreaming? Is this the rumble of age and sainthood? Let me say this. You can inspect the thundering skies for saliva. You can feed into the machinery of demolition. You can pledge your darkness to a joke.

But—my sweet, sweet beauties—brace yourselves. I'm going to look you in the eye."

If Armstrong was interesting the moon would blush into a fizzy paradise, florid with ease and wild good humor. The moon is as dry as a health cracker.

THE SIRI GUN

☼

"What were you doing in Washington, Atom?"

"Visiting my rights."

"Wiseguy, eh?"

"Where were you on June 16?" asked the second cop.

"Hiding a pod in the basement."

"Wiseguy," muttered the first, nodding.

Nice day—sunny outside and I hadn't bled much. I was sat in a yelling cell as a bullet lost its flavor in my leg. The two stooges had me jacked to a polygraph. I'd breezed the Wittgenstein controls and we were fronting off to beat the band.

"I get a phonecall? Need to send a singing telegram to my rabbi."

"You keep Northin' us Chief Blince'll tear you a new asshole."

"I need a new asshole—how soon can he get here?"

"You got a gun called a Glory Hand, Atom?"

I rolled a nicotine patch and lit it up. "Okay fellas, you got me. I'll tell it like it happened. Now let's see."

And I spun the following, beginning with my habitation of an office on Saints Street and nothing doing. People think my business is all swapping the clever with rich clients bathchair-bound in a hothouse of flycatchers and septic orchids. Missing daughters and like that. In fact I was just kicked back in contemplation when the phone rang. Siri Moonmute sounding wired.

Siri explained that she was now wanted for everything. She had never been into the perfect crime as she didn't go for Gautier's principle of virtue in correctness of form. I knew a girl could be perfect because of her flaws. The whole thing was subjective.

Siri was into purity—this it was possible to quantify. A pure crime is like a diamond in which no facet or depth is clouded by legality. It's criminally saturated, every move from start to finish creating a breach in legislation. This was a headcrime Siri had pondered increasingly of late and with laws entering the statute books at a rate of thousands per year, it was getting easier all the time. So she'd done it, packing as many offenses as possible into each second. Her name smeared the copnet like a rash.

Siri started in on how the difficulties of evading detection were no longer an inducement and she'd been hurting for a new challenge, at which I remarked if she wasn't careful she'd be sat cod-eyed in a bodyvan. Siri spoke in awe of the particle-science phenomenon of the *singularity*; a point at which all known laws break down. If a substance is supposed to expand, in a singularity it contracts. If light is meant to bend, in a singularity it's stiff as a board. Where laws are created to explain behavior these squirls occur every few months; but where laws are created to prevent behavior—as among people—they happen many times per second. The latter laws are patently inaccurate, and a pure crime is a statement of unmixed truth.

"Siri," I stated, "don't you understand that the cops will stick it in and break it off at a speed which will surprise everyone? Such pristine behavior as you display is the sole preserve of a mutant in a belfry."

Siri remarked that I had failed to gauge the full extent to which she was gung ho. She was chock full of that quality and would express it at the drop of a hat. "There was a point there, Atom, I'd set things up so that I was committing several hundred offenses in one instant, and I could feel the very atmosphere change—it was as though my misdemeanors had reached such a superdensity that they began to implode."

"Like a black hole, collapsing in on itself?"

"Exactly."

"How do you feel?"

"Like god. Could you come over?"

By the time I got there the area was under containment by the cops. Behind them a hole in space spiralled like the water spinning down a drain, a tornado of light sucking scraps of paper and nuggets of masonry out of view. The trooper boy Marty Nada stood at the cordon tape yelling through a bullhorn so I went to ask him the deal. He didn't bother to lower the bullhorn. "Oh hi Atom. Ah it's a singularity of some kind, its gravity so powerful not even lies can escape. We've lost five officers going near that thing."

"How'd it happen, they know?"

"Still guessing. Pun gun misfire? Etherics? Eschaton rifle'd do it, right person."

"Uh, okay thanks Marty."

"Sure Atom."

Well, another day another dollar. But it has a bearing upon what happened the following afternoon when I got an out-of-town yell from the Caere Twins. These bottle-bald cuties were crime stylists who monitored the scene for crimes that went outside the known taxonomy of offense. A wholly new crime was rare and precious as white gold. They were camped out in Washington with the theory that a target moved least at the axis. I split the border to face with them in an apartment so small they had to sleep in the mirror. The place really served as a digital gun foundry. Forcing the gun scene from industry to desktop, the Crime Bill had freed it up for limitless configuration. The Twins were among the many who innovated firearms on the fly.

"Siri sent an 'eyes only' letter," they chirped in unison. "With real eyes."

The Twins gave me some tech laced with sarcasm so heavily encrypted it never really thawed into effect. It was like being flogged with a double helix. I finally extracted the fact that Siri had sent them an e-mail just before her crescendo, but the feed had been jacked to their forge at the time and the message funnelled into a blank skeleton gun which had lain ready for impression.

"What was the message?"

"A command trail," they said. "Two million keystrokes."

"All this theory's like eating hair," I whined, impatient. Then the truth sunflared over my brainlobes—the only way to achieve the offense density Siri craved was to hack it, initiating a thousand thefts, frauds and intrusions in a split second. The program she created to do it now informed the design of the gun cooling in the Twins' forge. They opened the panel and retrieved a firearm resembling a tin ammonite with a chicaned barrel and pupstock Steyr grip. Spiral cylinders were real fashionable then. All part of life's kitsch tapestry.

"Etheric sampler in the butt," said the Twins. "This gat's her legacy and culmination, shadowboy, her tub of warm ashes. She'd want to be home."

"You mean I should take it back and scatter the ammo? No, not me. The cops are right about a gun eventually getting used whether or not there's a reason."

"True of them, shadowboy. Be careful."

My car had been replaced with an inflatable replica which burst when I put the key in the door. So I was on a clunker train to Beerlight. Carriage to myself until this big guy in gut braces bellies in. Looks at the empty seats, then lumbers right over to me, dropping down opposite. Regards me with a head like a throw cushion as the light and dark pass over us both.

"Staring is its own reward."

"It certainly is." In the pocket of my full-length void coat, the ammo-guzzler zinged against my palm.

"Shave the fuzz from the face of a moth, and what do you get?"

"Fatty Arbuckle?"

"Think again."

"You?"

"On the nose. Tubs Fontanel's the name. Fontanel by name, fontanel by nature. Retired cop but I keep my eyes open. Know why I consider myself always on cop duty?"

"Any impediment to imitation'd throw you back on your laboring character?"

"Nah. Watch this." He hauled himself up, stood in the aisle, and started throwing flat, startled shapes with his arms and legs. This galoot danced like a cartoon robot. Then he sat down, panting and chuffed. "Know where I learned to dance that way?"

"The laughing academy?"

"Nah." He took out what looked like a cell phone. "Know what this is?"

"Scrambler hotline to the circus?"

"Nah. Two-end scanner. I hear about a ventilation job I go round and scan the floor pattern. All began two years ago. I was flippin' through crime scene photos—you know, chalk body outlines on the floor? Got this flickerbook effect, like the outline man was dancin'. And I thought—get a choreographer in here, we're sittin' on a goldmine. Got dance numbers from every month last year. Multiple homicides I string together for, like, big production numbers. That thing I just did? Combination o' fifty crime scenes, January, central DC. I'm based in DC but I just hear about the fashionable events in Beerlight, yeah? Vortex, goofy crime scene, chalkline's a doozy, wanna record it. You from Beerlight? How's the local color?"

"Red."

"I get it. You got the chair there? We got gas in Washington. Folk say the killin' jar's just as cold-blooded as some homicides, but I think it's a crime of passion. Yeah rare's the day I forget to bless those who gave us a blank check on enforcement. Them and the bicthought media. Support us you're objective, criticize us you're biased. I could point to a dozen trite precedents. But the respect aint there. What happened to faith in a higher authority?"

"Burned in a wicker man?"

"Nah. Average Beerlighter's got a morality like a ferris wheel. What is it with you people? You hear me, boy? It'll be shuffleboard and orange walls before you realize you're runnin' naked through an alligator ranch. . . ."

His words had galvanized me into sleep—boredom was always the heaviest rock in the law's armory. And I dreamt I was a clown driving a dynamite truck. Cliff edges blurred like sawteeth. Siri was sat next to me in red-fleck dungarees. "What did the Twins say?" she asked calmly. "Was it more art than science or was it based on exacting principles?"

"C-c-can't you see I don't give a damn about that?" I shrieked, wrenching the wheel, and the tires blew out, waking me.

Tubs Fontanel was dressed the same as Siri from the dream, and looking as astonished as an inevitably snipered senator. Arterial blood misted and swirled between us, settling in a soft rain. I'd blown a hole in my thigh. The retired cop's bewilderment was perfectly apparent. "What the f . . ."

I bowed to his judgment so fast his nose broke. The train was grinding into the station. He was snuffling something about paraffin and death as I leapt to the platform and made for the barrier with a few dozen others. I included a bullet now, and a thin gore trail. Yelling behind me—I turned to see Tubs bent over, gasping, light falling into him and being extinguished. He was a vacuum. Through the barrier, feeling squirly.

As I crossed the concourse everything was incredibly high res. I could see infringement thresholds overlapping as people jumped queues, threw punches, glared—every head a poisoned chalice. Kirlian stormfronts collided around the rushing crowds. Mindmade law lines crisscrossed the air, weak and tangled as gossamer. As I passed through they shrivelled and vanished like burning hair. I stashed the gat in a locker, and blew.

Back at my barnacle-encrusted office I told the whole thing to my girlfriend and technical adviser, and she said it couldn't have been more Freudian if the gun had gone off as I went into a tunnel. I told her Freud was projecting, she kicked me in the balls and I blacked out for sixteen hours, waking only when the cops arrived.

"And that's how I ended up in a yelling cell with you guys," I told the two interrogators affably.

"So you wouldn't know why the President was found with his head in the mouth of an embalmed Kodiak bear. Utterly naked and quite dead. Five yards of Chinese firecrackers up his ass." They showed me photos of the crime scene.

"Can I keep these?"

"Atom, your story ain't even halfway good. And void without material proof. But we can bust open every last safe locker in Beerlight grand and if we find a gun, we'll do you as an accessory to the Siri job. We got you either way."

The cops soon decided my death was unnecessary—something I'd been thinking for years. I could have said anything and breezed the polygraph, the Siri bullet handling the conscience response. But it wasn't a heroic dose—the gunshot was accidental, motiveless, self-inflicted. No intent. The Twins were scornful.

Worst of all, the cops had the gun, though they didn't know it. There were a thousand lockers in Beerlight station, and a gun in every one.

INFESTATION

☼

Drella was told there was something wrong with her head. In the small shrill school, she alone could not understand. It was like being among a baffling, alien species.

Seemed she should learn to smile when she was unhappy, to stop laughing, to speak up, to never speak to strangers, to share guilt for the acts of strangers, that strangers made the laws of the land, that the laws of the land valued things over life, that life ended if a stranger decided it, to be where she could be found, to feel one thing and do another. How could she hang so many contradictions in one skull?

She asked questions and incited an anger far fiercer than that provoked by bullies or stupidity. Mrs. Rocust taught a religion of love and threatened to blot out Drella's sight with a pencil which she ticktocked from one iris to the other. The class laughed as one, seeing no anomaly. Their eyes were windows onto incoherence.

Rocust marched her out into the cold yard, where Drella felt relieved and peaceful.

Snow and night fell. The yelling kids were long since gone and Drella felt blissfully forgotten. The moon ghosted among clouds.

But Mrs. Rocust slammed from the schoolhouse, locking up loudly, and took Drella by the paw to drag her through the shuttered town. Down steps and alleys, under lamps threading with firefly snow. Until they neared a little shop with bower windows, lit up like a shop on a Christmas card. A single knock, and they were admitted.

The shop appeared to be a cobbler's or machinist's. The proprietor was a rosy-cheeked man who winked at Drella and bid her warm her hands at the fire. Mrs. Rocust lay her bag on the small table as Drella crossed the low-ceilinged room. The shopkeeper took hold of Drella's face, a scream smearing across his palm. Pushing her against the table, he hit her with a hammer until she was obediently still, then he and Mrs. Rocust secured her to the tabletop. Mrs. Rocust sat in a corner knitting as a broad drill bore a hole in Drella's skulltop and the shopkeeper drew out the contents. Brain sluiced along a drain like clotted milk. As knitting needles fiddled and clicked a metal keg and delivery tube were brought to bear upon the girl's open head. Hundreds of gleaming black spiders gushed down the pipe and filled the skull cavity. A few escaped, darting across the table before the wound was sealed over.

Back in school, there was nothing to be said. Hung in every skull was a ball of spiders muddling gleefully, lining the bonewall with an impenetrable web. Behind Drella's face was a roiling blizzard of little minds, without invention or comment. Inner contradiction was impossible. Her head felt fizzy but that only made her shout with the others.

Once she got a nosebleed which included a few spiders, and thought nothing of it.

BESTIARY

Albatross: expressionless, cruising bird. In *The Ancient Mariner* Coleridge hung a dead one around the protagonist's neck in a desperate attempt to make him appear more interesting.

Bat: this animal is harmless when found in a kidney tray.

Crab: write incriminating evidence on its back and see it run.

Dog: malevolent, n-shaped animal, which may sometimes be heard to speak.

Eel: hose and nozzle, moving in water.

Frog: rubber monster which stares openly at friend and foe alike.

Garter snake: a sacred animal in many tribes, the garter snake is best when roasted.

Hammerhead: large, inflatable shark. Only the fins, sneering mouth and tremendous size tell the common man that this is no ordinary pet.

Ichthyosaurus: prehistoric dolphin with hubcap eyes, first discovered by Mary Anning in Cornwall while she was dynamiting fish.

Jaguar: when provoked, this car will explode.

Knife: in cricket, the object one throws at a bastard.

Lizard: when mashed, this animal resembles snot.

Maggot: treadle-operated finger biscuit made mainly of beef.

Narwhal: elephant with dangerous, stabbing nose and dry sense of humor.

Octopus: doughy animal which, when removed from its ocean environment, is disconcertingly useless.

Penguin: black and white creature with a bill, often mistaken for a lawyer.

Quetzalcoatl: inflatable god of the Aztecs, known for its raised eyebrows and milk-giving shoulderblades.

Ribbonfish: elongated animal used by senior judges for self-flagellation. The fish is also used for the binding of wrists and in emergencies may be discreetly eaten.

Salami: zombie meat—leave it alone.

Trilobyte: thrown hard at a mime, this empty fossil shatters on impact.

Underwear: tight clothing worn by some federal agents.

Vampire bat: cute, pig-faced bird which drinks blood. The family *Megadermitidae* cannot drink blood and are called "false vampires." Which goes to show that if you're a bat, you can't win.

Whip: the ostentatious manner in which a public speaker discards his trousers.

Xylophone: percussion instrument made from vicars' ribs and played at high speed by circus clowns.

Yell: the manner in which one addresses a policeman.

Z particle: possessing a weak nuclear force, these particles are seen to bear a likeness of Orson Welles' face when viewed at 20mm resolution.

SAMPLER

"You're all brain and headlights Eddie. Your every move shows you're in love with your coat."

"So?"

"So you look like a student—stagger outta here talking shit no one'll slam an eyelid, it's perfect. They'll think you're quoting Baudrillard—the tedium is the message."

This from a bastard with hair like aerosol cheese. Head like a fire axe. Gob like a stick on trick. One-way staring eyes. Transfixed by dogma, you'd assume. But here in the University basement Kramer had pushed beyond the theoretical and was testing weird shit on kids too poor to have a center of gravity. The black hole of the philosophy department had swallowed a friend of mine. Now it ran around the nighttime boiler room checking light levels and adjusting dials on what looked like an iron lung.

"This the isolation tank?"

"Think of it as a particle accelerator—I ain't got all year to wait for you to come up. Just for the kickoff. You'll be testing a new drug every night Eddie. Some roll-over with the half-lives but I can adjust for it in the results, don't you worry."

"Jo told you I'm not much of a user."

"We're all users Eddie," laughed Kramer, checking the angle on one of the camcorders. "You know the Victorian explorer James Lee discovered Malay 2 in the jungles of Sumatra—called it the Elixir of Life. Seeds out of a pod plant, boiled up. Said the stuff nixed the effect of any drug in your system, got you straight in a half hour. Today we're so out of whack with chemicals inherent to modern life, if we dropped Malay 2 we'd get our first taste of what it is to be human."

"Got much?"

"Nobody'll back a hunt for it Eddie—too much money in the false war. Never came across any and I've got some fierce stuff, believe me." He grinned, slotting a cassette into a recorder. "American mainly. Them analog laws have fired the imagination of bathtub chemists coast to coast—theoretical highs, illegal before they exist and a regular challenge." He knelt and detached a grating from the wall, reached into the vent and dragged out a Samsonite case. "A substance like speed taken like grass, or stuff like ayahuasca but with no detectable indole and a snacktime half-life. Really something to shoot for, isn't it?"

"I guess."

He hefted the case onto a table and flipped the catch. "You guess." His laughter ricocheted around the basement like a bullet in a limo. "I like that. Jo said you were a clown."

"Where is Jo—haven't seen her for a bit."

"Around. We get started?" He took out a ghostlike baggy.

I had to remember Jo and that this was my amateur stab at a private investigation. I was hoping for a handle on the coming ordeal. Maybe I could forego the tolling spars and booming refineries of Hell and scare up a rosier revelation. But I was scared to pieces already. In Kramer's palm lay a weird seed. "What's that and what's it doing here?"

"A kind of sea onion."

"So small?"

"Only one layer, my friend. Fifth from the middle."

"So specific?"

"Bet your life."

"And the second half of the question?"

"Nothing. Until eaten by you, sunshine. Then you'll take a square look at your wounded life and tong out the bullet. It's a tryptamine indole like psilocybin. Compound eye of the soul. You know your *Flatland*? Nicked from Hinton? Just as a spherical object intersecting a 2-D plane appears out of nowhere as a morphing 2-D circle, the intersecting of a 4-D hypersphere into our 3-D continuum appears as a morphing 3-D lens-form, like a flying saucer."

"Or an old hat."

"I know, Eddie," Kramer laughed. "But I'm paying you to listen to this, right? And keep mum about our proceedings here—walls have ears. Or they will if you take enough of these. Chugalug."

I necked the stuff and washed it down.

"You're doing fine Eddie," Kramer said as I stripped and climbed into the sensory deprivation tank. I lay back and was floating in salt-dense water, feedback wires taped to my head. "I like to think of an experiment as a mound of dough booted off a high cliff, Eddie—it tends to develop a shape and momentum of its own. That's the real joy of it, see?" And he slammed the hatch.

Trad

I was hanging weightless in the pitch dark, Kramer's gear climbing the tree of my nervous system. Sensory input reduced to near-zero. No color, no sound worth a damn. Nothing happening. The eighties all over.

Sudden, massive anxiety. I'd been tricked. This thing was a time machine. This was 1983, I was sure of it. Sterility. Nothing. Didn't anyone see how boring this was?

I breathed deep—gusts filled the universe as I tried to reason calmly. Dead phases in history always had an end. Once even the dimmest of my generation realized we were growing in a vacuum, the logical course would be to fill it out ourselves. So at the decade's end there'd be a bleed of color composed of drugs, music and a weak stab at creativity.

Until then I'd just have to sit it out. Again.

Where did I get the idea the process would be accelerated? Rhomboids were turning in space—prisms dilating and shrinking as they thundered past in a wake of displaced molecules. The pinpoint pupils of a thousand stars stretched into lines of acceleration. Drawing slowly near was a massive rumbling something, an irony-intricate convolution, roiling endlessly into its center. I shot into the paunch of a cloud and a gush of cellular fluorescence unveiled the heart of the thing—nodular beings darting back and forth across a havoc lattice. It was like finding a microchip in an oyster. Enamel things like fridge magnets sped around a schematic warren of supercharged synthetic.

I was on the surface with them, meeting one. I could only assume its face was the first of its kind. It was like a badly-moulded trophy. Other marionettes barrelled over like rolling trashcans. There was nothing lifelike about them at all. I addressed them with all the calm of a cornered chef. "You're scaring the shit out of me and you bloody know it!"

Here my meaning was translated into a visual datacloud which bulbed in space between us. My meaning was so basic and unrefined, however, that the datacloud consisted merely of my own head, screaming in terror. In reply, one enamel goblin manipulated this image, tugging at the head's jaw. Its action translated as: "If both the skull *and* teeth are made of bone, why bother with gums?"

"There's a reason."

"Which is?"

"I *know* there's a reason."

"Do insects bruise?"

I was hemmed in by grinning, rampaging technical trolls, a robotic wrecking crew cracking up and reconfiguring with laughter. My head image was grasped, skin torn off like a hood—haywire quills riddled at last the neglected hemispheres of my brain. Mayhem by the numbers. Fierce carnivalia in a hectic paradise of blinding headaches and derision. They held aloft an alien relic of intensified experience. Its title was *Don't Take Your Eyelids So Seriously Billy Jean* and I was made to understand this was the "Book of Life."

"It *can't* be," I said, resisting with every burnt fiber. "Don't. Be. So. *Stupid*, man!"

Under the clanging stars they stood stock still to show me clearly that they were wearing checkered trousers and implicit in this act was the command that I should do the same and thus bear witness to the sacred dimensions. When I held fast they created a thoughtshape which made known that if I refused I would be placed inside a Charlie Chaplin movie and the resulting depression would mean the end of me. And as if to illustrate, the universe banged into a fixed, flat, black and white square into which a figure hung—Chaplin surely, doing some dismal stunt and expecting adulation. "Okay Eddie? You been screaming to beat the band in there."

My hands shot up at Kramer's throat and he pulled back, hauling me out of the isolation tank. As he wrestled free and staggered I saw the drug was still on line—the walls were like paper screens, the entire building a semi-transparent 3-D schematic. "Woah!" Kramer gasped. "Jo said you had a temper." From his mouth bulbed the ectoplasmic thoughtshape and it was Jo herself, saying: "Kramer lies. A bastard like that'll go tilling through your innards with a hook to find something amusing."

As Kramer moved I saw the fourth-dimensional part of the man receding from him like the ganglion behind an eye. This was the varicose root of his intentions and I glimpsed the shit-and-poison ugliness of it an instant before the drug cut out.

Back at the flat, I felt like the bug that awakes to find it's turned into a clerk. Sick, the clock snipping away at me. Lie in the dark till there's no hard feelings. Except I wasn't allowed that kind of time.

Grail

"Religion is the opium of the people Eddie," Kramer smiled, dumping grey powder into a blender and replacing the lid. "And it's cheaper." He flipped the switch and the contents blurred.

"What's this."

"Ecclesiastical pharmacology. Pounded holy relic. Dried and sifted saint. Either it works or the Bible's shit my friend."

"The ashes of people?"

"Are dangerous to your health when prepared correctly. But don't worry your sticky little head about that. Skulked from a ransacked tomb with these dry beauties. Seb and Wolfgang in there. As a bridge I've buffered in 10,000 mg of piracetam and the pestle powder from these." He held up what looked like a couple of chalk stubs.

"What are they."

"The horns of an otherwise useless giraffe. Weird eh?" But his voice indicated that he didn't think it weird at all.

I swallowed the mixture—it tasted like rust or herbal tea. "How much active ingredient?"

"What I term a 'recognition of the problem'."

"Which is?"

"A thousandth of a percent of the solution."

In the tank, watching the cohering shapes of the trip waft through the darkness. A panoramic glide over life's accidental parameters, heart fluttering in the updrafts. There was something in the stale stuff after all. A continent taking form.

A one-note recurrent heaven receded like astroturf. I'd thought it would broil and change but this was chronic. Statue people were fixed in it as though in quick-dry cement. Stuck out of the jigsaw edges were antique moralities, justifications severed and flapping. Denizens merely glanced as if I were part of the landscape, an overhang of mild effrontery.

The weirdly cruise controlled tour continued—all that had been denied in heaven was coming into view. Convolute slang channels emptied into deep ocean. Suspicion was sumptuously tiding and receding. Polychrome components drifted like dead sea fruits. Molecules of invention flurried in jubilance, the air candied with unbound personality. The sea became a waterfall which tumbled and thundered relentlessly upon an infinite bruise—the soft fontanel of god's mistakes. I added myself at once to its efforts, hurling downward—and like Alice descending the well I noticed a diverting strata in the walls I was passing. Here was all the righteous indignation denied the devout, the romping rebellion repressed by the humble, the gene memory of sarcasm. Imagine the message I could take back with me. Four million years of concentrated scorn locked in the DNA of contemporary man. The fossil record alone must be stacked with tableaux of piss-taking neanderthals. Ancient put-downs long since forgotten. Think what we could learn from the coelacanth. I heard reverberations from the inner sanctum of hilarity. If this didn't constitute enlightenment I couldn't imagine what would.

It was like waking up before you hit the ground—I was about to plunge through god's skylight skull when the trip cut out. Tearing urgently at the feedback leads, I clambered out of the tank.

The room was all turbulent fiery red—Kramer was ponced up, transformed. Hooves like cloth irons, a black coat, a nose full of teeth, fluorescent eyes and a tangle of horns from here to the ceiling. This guy thought he was some kind of reindeer.

"Hatrack antlers eh?" I boomed, beefed up and pounding with heroic energy. "The universe proceeds from my nostrils."

Religion did two more things for me—it allowed me to rig up a satire-activated psychic snare anchored to Kramer's chakra points and, in blurring the boundary between fact and fiction, allowed me to believe satire could have an effect in the world. After what seemed like hours of eloquence in which I scorched home the notion that he didn't know where his soul ended and his tailoring began, Kramer simply responded: "You've a lot to learn Eddie—the stitches aren't out on your childhood."

And he played back the video of my repartee, in which I merely sat like a furless rat, eyes hooded, whispering the word "vengeance" in every language and dialect ever known to humanity.

Gutter

I felt as dead as an airplant and the secret agenda I'd been guarding escaped me. Had someone I knew had an accident? "You're deep enough in we don't need the tank anymore Eddie. Lie on the stretcher here and I'll hook up the EEG."

I lay staring at the basement ceiling.

"See this bug Eddie? Nanotech—a thousand micromachines embedded in a silicon substrate. We're talking media memes, my friend, program-specific neural adjusters in a chitin-coated intramuscular pill, or tabloid. Acts like a parasite forcing you to feed the disease. Hatches the royal eggs of hypocrisy in your skullcase. Renders conversation a grotesque carnival of rearlit generalities, just the way you like it."

"Have I taken it yet?"

"Has he taken it yet—I like that. Let's say you have and the next one's on me eh?"

"How many can I take without risk?"

"None. But I'll give you some free advice if you have a bad time and live."

"It's a deal."

He put a carpenter's rivet gun to my arm and banged the trigger. "Make a fist Eddie."

For a while I listened to the brain damage circling its place, the windblown public telephone of my chattering teeth. Black static was blizzarding, volatile and irrelevant. Then I was side-swiped into a commotion of whirlwind supposition and lazy equivalence, trying to get a fix on stability in a vortex of perpetually recoiling space. I found myself hungering for the wooden stone at the heart of the peach, a truth which didn't change from one moment to the next.

Then I was rawboned in emptiness, slowly formulating screams in the vacuum. Grey erosion under a gutless sky. Sat around me were dry dupes wired securely into a powerhouse of contradictions. The expedient distortions of the local morality made it near impossible to concentrate on a single object, but I homed in on one guy bound and gagged between binary apprehensions, receiving regular shocks to which he could only concur. I was embalmed in the man, seeing through his eyes, and before him a grey screen was flashing TAX SHOCK— BABY SHOCK—WAR SHOCK—ROYAL SHOCK—and so on every few seconds. And though he reacted to each with a clench and moan, it was muscle deep. He didn't know he was only pretending.

I craned my neck up at an endless hierarchy of bullshit, gargoyled and stratified, runnelling with toxins. Sentient junk flowed around me like poison. Armed with nothing stronger than my innocence, I was filled to the marrow. Here knowledge was a hot potato passed on rather than downed and digested. An argument as thin as a mouse's bellyskin was unassailable. Anyone who grew his own mind was diminished, voiceless and futile under lofty neglect, incinerative condescension and the derisive intimacy claimed by government, which I now perceived as an artificially low, spike-frame ceiling an inch above us.

Then a real shock went through me—I'd rolled off the stretcher onto the floor. The basement was blear, flat, doomed. I saw a beef skeleton walking through it. Kramer put a thermometer in my eye and measured my screams. "Like your style

Eddie," he said, then held up an inkblot card. "What do you say this is?"

"A mirror?"

"Any feelings of paranoia?"

"Why? Who sent you? Are you recording this?"

"You know I am."

"Don't stare at me," I breathed in gusts of demented outrage. "Don't *ever* look at me!"

"I'll sit over here Eddie."

Like that of a frog his face was fixedly sarcastic and masked whatever scheming transpired there. One minute you're thinking it's the cutest frog you ever saw, the next it's bitten your cheek and pulled you headfirst into the blood-foaming swamp. "And no one to help you," I announced in the smudgy video playback the following night, my image twitching like a NASA monkey. "Just the screaming and the hollering and the burning knowledge that you could and should have avoided the entire situation. Meanwhile the Germans have sucked your underpants out the back of the dryer and created a clone out of your DNA, a clone which commits crimes for which the police put out a warrant for *your* arrest, while the underpants are fired into orbit from a circus cannon."

Kramer watched without comment, his ghoulish equilibrium worse than any put-down.

"That's right!" shouted the madman on the screen, neckcords straining with assertion. "The insidious theme-parking of the drugscape in this nation is only a part of it! Expanding— yeah, right! The universe is made of erectile tissue and we're *headed* for the big bang, baby! We're going *nova* baby!"

Kramer paused the machine mid-rant, my face a blurred gnash. "Good work, Eddie—rope *that* off and charge admission eh? Just a second now and I'll get tonight's drop."

I watched him open a plastic ice box, trying to keep the hunger and fascination from my face. The room was fizzing with psychostatic and the spinal joys of persecution mania. I noticed an EEG printout was still in the machine from the previous night, and took a look—instead of the scratched bandwidth of fluctuating brainwaves it bore a headline: DOPE TRIALS DEATH SHOCK. Reading that stuff could rot your brain. When I looked again, the sheet was blank and Kramer was calling me over.

"A mind's the most controlled substance there is Eddie." He'd lifted a melon-sized something from the ice box, its detail blurred in cellophane.

Small greys

"We all know about Roswell 1947 and the little grey space guys, but what the average Joe doesn't suspect is that alien neurochemistry is biocompatible with our own and, when properly preserved, can be eaten like pistachio ice cream."

"Why all the talk, Kramer? Just gimme the stuff."

"No, really—it was a tradition among the ancients that the strength and wisdom of their fathers could be ingested through cannibalism of the brain and other organs, and studies of treated neuroplasm have provided confirmation. Take a look at this beauty." He had finished stripping away the wrapping and on the table between us was a severed grey domer with pursed lips, flick-knife ears and the dead eyes of a shark. He used a cranial ridge as a slimline handle to lift away the skullcap like a casserole lid. "Forty-seven's a top vintage Eddie—tuck in."

It tasted like pasta, or worse. Already sensing its slow but fierce insinuation into myself, I spooned the lubricious grey matter and watched the dead head. The room was blotting, holes opening in the air. Bits of wall and the grinning Kramer were dropping out like jigsaw pieces, a brittle facade beyond which cascading protozoan and microbial life bloomed into lagoons under an aching blue sky.

Field conditions here were so aggressively lethargic I immediately surrendered, stretching an eyelid between two angels to use as a hammock. Oases beclustered with sex spores, trance lakes of slow automatic fish, heady heated asphalt, fluttering octane clouds, ramparts, noon-blue apples, gusts of thick air swirling with chemical particulates of know-it-all elixir, each watery narcotic drench leaving me as happy as a dog in a sidecar. Contracting red rubrics cruised over, clicking into place on a reef of beautiform coral. All framed by curlicues of languid abraxia. It was so graphic, this nonstop everyplace, I forgot what I was waiting for, who I was meant to be. This went on, for years, what with one thing and another.

Finally, when I was admiring a sundial in some pillared cloud temple, its triangular hand became the fin of an approaching hammerhead. The fin sliced the landscape like a knife through a movie screen, exposing a darkness I could never have imagined. I wandered through to explore this gloom and gradually recalled that this was Earth, the basement, Kramer. Determined to remember what I'd learned in paradise I scrawled revelations with the urgency of a novice. The next day I awoke with a rubber forehead and the following distilled gospel:

1. Armadillos are simply dogs in chainmail.
2. Never roast a farmer. If you think they complain under normal circumstances, you don't know the half of it.
3. When a man drops his wife's dish, the universe opens for a moment like a lion's jaws.

4. Underwater, punch force is reduced.
5. Each sneeze frees a hundred lawyers.
6. At every action ask yourself, "Why feel ineffectual when my very frustration advances the world cause?"
7. One thing is sure to hasten celebration—the death of a waiter.
8. Always remember the cat when shoving a bastard off balance.
9. At day's end, surrender gracefully your trousers.
10. My belch will shake down your monuments.

It was like a new age solve-all by some LA cadet who never worked a day in her life. Except that these were rules you could live by.

Well pleased, I tilted across a flat which was breeding meaning in corners. Standalone peptides drooled down the walls. In the bathroom, my reflection looked back at me as though from the belly of a wicker man. A bony scaffold and hubcap pupils were surmounted by a halo of resentment. It was Jo's look. She'd sit in a chair, shop-dummy white, breathing through her bruise of a mouth, drugs echoing in the universe of her blood. At night she'd go out again—and come back worse. Then she didn't come back.

How long since I started in with Kramer? Four days? A year? Had he even paid me? What had I got? Nothing but the shabby notoriety of having stuck my oar into an adjacent dimension.

But I needed it. My soul was shrinking, depleted. Medulla brainlights burst around me like flak. I stumbled into the living room and glugged down the contents of a lava lamp. A yawn monster swelled out of the wall and faded immediately.

Big blues

"The universe works on a principle of cycles of improvement, my friend," Kramer stated, standing between two smocked-up surgeons. "Reincarnation shifts us upward through the species and finally the dozen or so human lives allotted us. We're not allowed to remember our past lives or the lessons learned there—a system so patently stupid a number of souls suicide out of each and every incarnation as a protest."

"Whatever it is get on with it."

"But here's the capper Eddie—by the last incarnation a pro-tester's retina becomes calibrated to contraband altitudes of despair and clarity." He laughed amiably. "I'll tell you Eddie, there's a wound so deep that when knitted by scar tissue it bisects the subject. Maimed isolation, mate of mine—it's a quick and easy procedure." A gas mask was clasped over my face. "I've every faith in you Eddie."

I woke in the clenched center of a scorpion headache. I was back at the flat, days or hours later. Crawling into the bath-room. Splashing water. In the mirror, a face bottle blue with bruises. Black stitches around the eyes like the lashes of a rag doll. And they weren't my eyes.

The flat atomized into cinder drifts and dark dunes. From horizon to frying horizon scissor insects labored toward anni-hilation. I saw with sulphurous clarity that the turning Earth was a turbine of evil, dumping forever its payload of horrors.

But I observed this punishing panorama as though sat beneath the bone sky of another world. Contusions the size of galaxies were nothing to do with me, except that I might be hospitalized in a trance of disinterest. I was now all shell. I had attained a state of pure irony. Cold static howled through me. Everything had died unmourned.

Scorched beyond identity, I crawled out of the bathroom. While I was gone a swarm of fluorescents had assumed responsibility for filling the living room. With the smell of burning hair and a bandwidth buzz, an oceanic face of rippling milk was swirling out of the wall. "Jo."

"Sweet of you to notice."

"How'd you get in the wall?"

"Sometimes the needle sucks — Kramer had this theory about people being a drug which has the world under its influence. I'm here there and everywhere."

"Why'd you let it go so far? Do you know your face is melting like wax? You're as big as the whole place — everything's shot to hell, I can't handle it."

"Are you finished — quite finished? For a start think of the shit you wrote the other night — remember? Your ego hit the powerlines. A drug revelation's a philosophy that's been yanked too young from its mother's tit. And there's no contest between dignity and junk, lover — Kramer's experiment depends on it."

"He'd need a control though — someone who hasn't taken the stuff."

Her eyes blinked, ripples spreading outward. "He's the control, you moron. Only a knife'd separate the halfshells of the bastard's dishonesty."

And I thought I'd avoided all this in rejecting further education. I stood, resolved.

Jo's face broiled, shifting. "What are you going to do?"

Everything

I popped the grill cover and stuck my arm inside — the case was there. At the table, I flipped the catches and started building a hit beneath the bare lightbulbs of the boiler room. Tryptamine, grail, memia and brain preserve, pressed into a dozen silicon substrate pills and loaded into the rivet gun. I had a headache like a white sky.

Noise and bluster at the door. I crammed myself in behind the boiler.

". . . You'll be testing a new drug every night Wally. Some roll-over with the half-lives but I can adjust for it in the results, don't you worry."

"You know I'm not much of a user."

"We're all users Wally . . ." Kramer's voice trailed away. He'd seen the case.

I stepped out. Standing hesitant by Kramer was an empty kid with a doorknob head. I levelled the rivet gun. "Go." He looked to Kramer for help, got none, and left in a hurry.

"You were meant to wake up tomorrow Eddie," Kramer said, tilling vaguely through the paraphernalia on the table. "I would have been there to greet you."

"I had help."

"I trust you not to call the police Eddie—I truly trust you. In these times of ours that's worth a great deal, more than you can know right now."

Did he think I was too sick and out of it to see his game? He was right—he turned and threw a fistful of grail dust in my face. My faculties exploded like Chinese firecrackers. Imprisoned in the maze of my own ears, I shouted for release.

Then I was after him with the gun, up the stairs and pushing through students as blank as a form. But it was midnight and these were ghosts of failure. I was tolling like a cracked bell. Deep pathologies opened up along every hallway.

Kramer was out across the tire-screech street, the city full of history smoke. A bus reared past me, alien portholes lit with spectators. Rain was blistering the streets. Kramer's shadow rippled over ribs of rotting architecture. London was sinking, and always had been.

I cracked off a shot and hit a dog, which exploded with a backfire. Two more shots whizzed past Kramer, another hit a stoplight and stuck like gum. I kept plugging at the retreating figure, and slowing. As I followed down an alley I began sinking into the ground, which had turned to sludge. I was wading, fell flat on my face.

"Life's a landscape of delay Eddie," Kramer said. He was standing over me. "You get this with your new eyes. Oh you can never have too much surgery my friend. And the arcane pharmaceuticals in bud behind those eyes—what independence could compete? Shove it out and let it grow a coat, Eddie. You'll have a charmed existence treading monastery ways paved with peanut brittle and the mere inconvenience of bleeding from the lungs till death steals the breeze from your gob. Would I sell you a wooden lemon?"

A buzzing atom of objectivity would have shown it was a crap argument, being based on the notion that freedom was feasible. But I had in me religion's guilt, revelation's wire, and the media's consensual distortions, frauds which needed feeding.

Kneeled on the wet ground, I raised the rivet gun to my forehead. "For what we are about to believe—"

The city went up in a psychic inferno, buildings swatted into typhoon blurs. I was looking down on the proceedings from atop a building—fluorescence eating across the map. "We escaping up here?"

"No, boy—this here's the Canary Wharf tower, see?" He turned me to look up the gradient of the pyramidal roof. We were stood on the rain-lashed ledge beneath it. He began dragging me through gale-force terror up the dark slope, yelling. "Forget what you've heard about Chartres and Masonic altars,

Eddie—this pyramid's the endpoint of a quantum-bore needle channelling earthline energies and shite from the five directions! Fall on the sword and you inject the whole fucking world!"

We'd reached the summit, altitude turbulence thundering the structure. Rain runnelled down the incline. I held my hand before my face—I was glowing like a halogen lamp. Beyond, the city was ash beneath a meat sky.

Then I was clung in panic, torn by skywinds. This was really happening. What was I doing here? Kramer stood easy a way off strobing in the pinnacle light, admiring the horizon. "Kramer! Too much!"

"Have I ever let you down Eddie?"

"Yes! And my name's not Eddie!"

I slipped, slamming onto the roofpoint.

Heartbomb shock. Screams stretching in a biochemical supernova. I blurred down the center well of the silver tower and hit the earth, blooming outward like a depth charge—duped. My soul blushed across the planet and seeped into the pores. I was with Jo and others, a part of me in the world's every atom, here there and everywhere. I was a drug, and I'd been injected.

It's hot and cold here, carnal red and cool green, stone dead and fizz-grid creative. Human beings tickle across the surface, but won't for long.

TAIL

"A hundred percent of marriages end in divorce, disappearance, or death."

She didn't respond right off and it was the only pause on a face that spread outward from her nose like a pond ripple. Since entering my barnacle-encrusted office she'd deployed a battery of behavioral ticks and swerves to draw the onlooker's emotions. She looked like a trapper twitching in her own snares. "Do you mind if I smoke?"

"Within reason."

She pulled a gasper and played some games. If she found a spider in the bath she'd probably flirt with it. "I know you're a busy man, Mr. Atom. I noticed, when I entered, the space exploration you were doing with your eyes. But I can't tell you what I'm going through. In today's climate one can't be too careful."

"There's a guy who knew how to keep trouble at a distance." And I pointed to a book on the shelf—*The Moon is Hell* by John

W. Campbell. "We all have our little devices. I myself build ana-
condas out of gelatin. But you're beckoning the future with
one hand and fending it off with the other. This fiancé of
yours—ain't he trustworthy?"

"He's not at all violent."

"That isn't quite what I asked, but we'll let that slide. He got
any bad habits you know about?"

"He doesn't kiss the humidor, if that's what you mean."

"Which course of exhaustion does he favor?"

"I believe he's an accountant."

"Uh-huh. And you want me to dog what I can only describe
as his steps."

"I know what you must think of me, Mr. Atom."

"Lifeless and privileged."

"Uh . . . well. But you see, Mr. Atom, I must proceed with
both eyes open. A premarital status report is a vital prerequisite
to a marriage. You do understand, don't you?"

I lifted my face off the desk to indicate attention. "It's jake
with me. But it'll take a lotta caperwork."

"If it's a case of money—"

"A case of money'll do fine. I'll pick it up tomorrow and get
to work."

"How long will you need?"

"Twelve of your Earth hours. Excluding toilet time. Don't
worry about a thing."

*Subject proceeded north up Valentine. Likely some nutrition in them
shoes. A swagger in his stride but his reflection in the store windows
told a different story, consisting of an entire mariachi band. The subject entered the Delayed Reaction Bar and showed a magenta infec-
tion to the regulars, provoking loud laughter. He upset a punnet of
shrunken heads which scattered like marbles across the floor. Subject*

*then shouldered his way through the crowd, all present slapping him
on the back and calling him "Bonky." He took the stage and began
unfolding animals, inflating them until they resembled balloons. The
barman presented him with a trophy which glinted like the lips of a
newly-dredged carp and the subject thanked all present with fond,
rheumy eyes. He spoke of "retribution" and "our enemies." He spoke
of a "great fire."*

*Subject proceeded northeast and stopped on the corner of Cale,
puffing his cheeks like a map cherub. Leering at old ladies, he stabbed
a child with a candy cane and ran, shouting something about "the
beginning." A great deal of shrieking was done at this time. The word
"thorax" was used several times. Subject took a table in a restaurant
and loudly and repeatedly referred to it as a "gob shop" until, heck-
ling the heavens with his laughter, he was ejected from the premises.
Subject pranced on the spot, emitting a mysterious clatter like a dime
in a slotpig. Entered market, approached fish stall and belted a flounder with a snow shovel, then staggered to his knees, sobbing loudly.
"Already dead, fella," a circle of mongers assured him gently. "Dead
already." Subject crawled under fruit stall and rolled onto his back,
kicking upward three times before he was dragged out. Capering
chase through market, baskets overturned, doves uncaged, escape
through traffic.*

*Subject stood on a bucket and shouted at passersby: "I am in that
temper that has no philosophy. I toast my aversions on a dark grill
and keep rage at bay through sheer patience and vandalism. Hand
in hand, pleasures land armies in my garden. Warm paws sound in
the street. How? Anyone can do it. When something is newly forbidden by law it is inevitably delayed by several minutes. See the release
of food against the night and kill the lousy cooperator. When charm
withers, invent some persecution and weep while leaving. It can't
hurt, and it always amuses. Press unexpected lips to blue jaws. You
deny it madam? Here's the hairy heart of a man, eh? Anything my*

*legs can pass, I'll ignore. I make my ass a party to every kind of
extravagance. Grazing on fashion is the mark of a patriot." The subject hailed US supremacy in yearly worldwide arms sales. "Ten billion
dollars worth to non-democratic governments alone. And that's
excluding torture stuff like this." And he fired a net gun at a street
mime. Rocked by 60,000 volts, the hapless performer reeled into a wall,
his head flattening down so that he looked like Gary Bauer. Subject
repeated the phrase "Check it out!" at high volume thirty-five times,
and then stated that "The gorilla was chuckling. It's a gadget. It has
features. We enter the rainforest. As I speak I'm beseiged by geother-
mals. Get me out of here." The unspoken content of his diatribe
yellowing the air, he dived through the crowd, throwing dog toys at
their feet and setting them into a frenzy of capitalist greed.*

*A goat passed, driving a hearse. The subject changed into a smock
and pants of blue linen as the hearse circled back and he climbed
aboard, saying "Try to be a leftover." Tailed subject, who proceeded to
high-tech underground lair on fringe of town. Subject distributed
tasks to rogue's gallery of assassins, removed glove to reveal steel hand.
Breezily inspected squadron of cropdusters in booming hanger.
Pounded pink dough in a wooden vat, bellowing with laughter. Lectured a silent henchman with the words "Limp and abundant we
dream of approval, reacting to two-octave orders with alacrity. Man
travels between pains in a rental, eh? Silent as a spider drying in a
cup. Yes, heroism decreases under inspection." He removed his glasses,
drew the pins from his hair and shook out the locks in a golden tum-
ble about his bare shoulders. "Initiate self-destruct sequence. This foul
planet is mine."*

*Donning a flowing black dress, subject proceeded past giant illu-
minated map of world dotted with missile symbols and descended wet
stone stairs through compressed strata of snot, latex, bone, and lard
into scabby fire-lit grotto, kneeling before giant horned baby made of
granite. Baby's eyes clanged open and booming voice stated it was*

"well pleased." Subject made a throne of demon's lap and began growing luminous beard at accelerated rate to beating drums. Strange, sightless creatures—moloks, I suppose—wailed in the catacombs and worshipped him as their god. Writhing celebration followed, freakish shadows heaving in the firelight. Subject fell to eating human flesh, roaring "Devil I am! Devil I am!" through a crimson grill of fangs.

"How's the coffee?"

"Just awful." She picked at her handbag and some kind of furry hat. "Oh, Mr. Atom, I've been so worried."

"You sittin' down, Miss?"

"What kind of detective are you—you can see I am." She twitched at a cigarette, fiddling. "Well? Did you follow him?"

I leaned back, leisurely. "I did."

"And?"

Outside, a distant cop car sirened like a whale.

"Everything checks out. He's clean as a whistle. Marry the man."

SHIFA

Before Beerlight got really bad it was a city of strangers. Few people knew each other well enough to get seriously mad. But as with all cultures at all times, there was a subculture which anticipated a trend. This is what the cops, amid the jostling of press conferences on the precinct steps, termed a "rogue social element." Communication was a cult to which, when the cultural histories were written, everyone would claim they had belonged from the beginning.

One of the forces to bring it into the mainstream was Doctor Albert Shifa. Author of *Know the Futility and Do It Anyway*, he specialized in aggression therapy. He advised angry men to strike pillows and other soft furnishings all innocent and unawares until the fury subsided. Learning thus that rage could be taken out on targets irrelevant to its cause, most of his patients went on rampages more randomly destructive than the Basra Road bombing.

Though troubled, the doctor persevered until he had occasion to treat the hitman Brute Parker, one of the fiercest bastards in the state. Parker thought he wanted to calm down some after a painful affair with the judgement angel Aggie Swan. As Parker lay on the couch, wound tight as a deep sea service cable, Doctor Shifa told him there was no need to take out the old graphic equalizer at the nearest and dearest opportunity. "No call to decline into murder and ridicule, Brute."

"It's me who is lookin' into the guns, Albert Shifa."

"Sure it is, I'm sure. You ever take off them aviator shades Brute?"

"In my dreams. But there's flyin' camels there too, so it don't seem too likely."

"Flying camels, crikey. That's as much and a little more than I can absorb today, Brute. I'd like you to try some relaxation and containment techniques. Take this piggy bank home with you. It's like a swear box except in this case you put a dollar in every time you want to shoot someone."

"This will save me enough for ammo."

"No, Brute—you miss my point."

"You think I'm dumb."

"Easy, tiger—I'm just trying to set you straight."

"No, you're workin' an angle. What else, I gotta wear sew-on mittens?"

"That's right—sit up, breathe deep—"

"I'm gonna kill."

"Count to ten, Brute, give yourself pause—"

Parker did count to ten, yelling each number at a louder volume, advancing on the doctor, shuddering to beat the band, fists like wrecking balls, veins bulging like inner tubes, backing him into a corner until at ten the explosion of multiphonic bellowing heard from the doctor's office made it known that Parker was a troubled man.

Following scenes of patient-straddled chest-pushing gurney rides and stand-clear heartshock, the doctor awoke in a state of trussed-up mummydom, and sensing that he had a visitor, turned his eyes painfully to the side.

"Hello Albert Shifa. I have brought grapes in a bag."

"Parker," snaffled Shifa, muting his alarm, "er you shouldn't be here. The police—"

"I have come here to thank you for my treatment Albert Shifa. You made me mad and I beat you all to pudding. This is as it should be, simple and direct. Never again will I take out my anger on those innocent of its cause. God bless you Albert Shifa." And he walked out, taking the grapes with him.

And so Shifa developed his direct action theory. Why take it out on pillows when the real cause was out there? No longer was his office a blizzard of feathers and injustice. Pop Joey conferred a lead safe upon Gilly Charmers from a height of forty-seven feet. Teddy Beltway shot the life out of Clinton Marks Deal in what he described as his "own small way." Gilbert Wham gave Chad Viagra an upward view of the bay. Hammy Roadstud dispensed so many bullets he started selling advertising space on the casings. Ban Saliva even used "doctor's orders" as a defense when arrested for feeding pasta to the chef responsible. Rain was washing away tears and sidewalk brains, and it was Doctor Shifa who found himself in the perjury room with the cod-eye a real possibility. His defense attorney was Harpoon Specter, whose back was still healing from the slapping it received after his last case—defending Parker. Out of superstition Harpoon hadn't washed or changed his clothes since. Every gesture of this unshaven bum corrupted the air.

His closing argument was a weeping sore of mitigation. "Murderous rampage? Easy for them to say. We've all felt that gun eruption coming up like a sneeze. Don't deny it. Add to that the knowledge that liberty is seldom reasonable and never innocent. Why take a chance? So we put the unearthly boot in, of course we do. Al Shifa made them do it? By what authority? Haven't they minds of their own? Well let's suppose, for argument's sake, that they haven't. What's left but raw bloody violence? And let's face it, they're a dab hand. Gilbert Wham once conducted an interesting rampage in which he punched anyone who'd stand still for it—and several who wouldn't. Yet by his own testimony today we've heard how Al here turned him around. Chad Viagra knifed Gilbert, Gilbert drowned Chad, and there for them the matter ended. You might even say that Chad exhibited somewhat of a victim psychology. And that random violence, thoughtless and unfocussed, is mere masking behavior. Excuses which leave us idle? Occam's Razor—the simpler the truth, the more painful it is to swallow. We must, according to Cicero, study each thing in the most perfect example we have of it. Let us take the man in the street. Beseiged from all sides by violence and the splintered systems of authority. His eyes are bulging, his face is weird, his pants are the color of clouded jade. He sweats like a bastard. Yells torrents of abuse at small, skittering dogs. Smothers himself with lard. And yes, if wronged, he kills. What do we expect, after all? We are forever and impossibly surprised. Look at the 2K bug—even when a disaster makes an appointment we're not prepared. And we call ourselves the masters of our planet. Yes, ours is the seething diamond mine of the stars. What are we but knots of oxygen?"

"Speak for yourself, Mr. Specter," spat the judge, exasperated. "I don't know if you've gone batshit crazy or if my grasp of our beautiful language has turned all to pus but for god's sake stick to the shocking facts—the retinal bars of my migraine are giving me ideas about you."

"Thank you your honor. The question before you is a simple one, ladies and gentlemen of the jury. In suggesting that these poor morons kill the objects of their rage rather than an innocent bystander or even some stuffed effigy, did the doctor offend? This government has taken the law into its own hands—very well, then let the punishment fit the crime. Instruct by your example, and see if this doesn't leave you satisfied. The denizens of Beerlight are desperate. Why should their desperation be quiet?"

"For peace," said the judge.

The jury decided the doctor was guilty as hell. But someone in authority had taken Specter's words to heart. At the killing hour, twenty grim spectators gathered to watch the electrocution of a pillow.

THE PASSENGER

Trying to figure out the difference between a model citizen and a crash dummy. Turning to one. "Heard the song, the song 'Be a Clown'? Could there be any darker exhortation to evil and chaos than that? 'Be a Fucking Clown'?"

Looking at the wall—I was bang up against the hero door. At the center of this was a porthole providing easy viewing for the lucky passenger with a head the size of an apple. On the ceiling were gills with the added conceit of a switch for varying the aperture. Only the crew knew what we were really touching in our innocence. I'd finally gone the whole way for the band.

The Beige Kidneys were a languid corrosion, if you'd just listen to them. If you'd just. Especially the newer stuff like "Ostrich Commandment" or "No Need to Inhale a Cookie." Or that break in the middle of "Incredible Mother" when we all started mumbling we were giving up—then a segue into laughing nuns. Great.

We'd turned every trick in the book to get heard. Edible discs. Skin-deep cajolery which barely wrapped the skull of our desperation. Faked-up bestiality snaps at which even the dogs laughed when we mentioned blackmail. Physical threats we'd wind up having to carry out tearfully and against our true nature. No go. Last resort was to down a plane and play a demo in the cockpit during the nose dive. When the black box was retrieved, at least three tin-kickers would hear the playback. Three, maybe four—and with luck the news. And as front man here I was, elected for sacrifice. Life's full of shit and surprises.

The black box—why wasn't the whole plane built to be so invulnerable? "Can't you see," I said to my neighbor, "there's hundreds of people here with us sitting in the smallest, tiniest chairs that, that legally qualify for the term up here? Or any-where? Or *anywhere?*"

How long before everyone knew I was ten bees short of a swarm? Before my understanding of this life took up residence beyond someone else's slack face and there gained some value? Well, I still had my motor skills.

One of the band had told me the soul was left behind during high-speed travel—took hours to catch up with the body and that was the cause of jetlag. Even suicidal roof-jumpers left their chewed souls up there—high buildings were forever haloed with circling wraiths. So maybe some echo of me might remain. My luggage in the hold contained enough nitrotex to find out. This was it.

My appearance in the aisle lost the element of sudden drama as everyone else in the row also had to step out, but once I was established there and everyone had regained their seats I raised the little short-range detonator. "Alright everyone take it easy!"

A Captain's announcement crackled over the speakers—big mistake, luggage on wrong plane, heading for Australia. I could see my bomb winding up on a bleached carousel with skeleton horses. There's life, right there. Amid groans of disappointment I negotiated my way back to the seat.

A few hours of standard-issue bile and something, yes, at first imperceptible. The thwarting of my crap scheme had begun in me a slow transition from one configuration of impotence to another. We'd discussed technicalities and statistics when we were saving for the ticket—now it all came back to me. Cast-iron figures of one jam-smear for every million departures and they still put up enough to kill 1,500 captives per year. "Chant the odds all you want," I hissed to my neighbor. "For those poor fools it's *one hundred percent*, understand me?"

He glanced up and then back to his meal. Food here was rubberized, manually inflated, but deliberately too small to keep me afloat in the freezing Atlantic. Over there a fat guy looked like he had a parachute packed in his mouth. Come to think of it my nose felt stuffed to the limit. Miraculous salvation? Or would I snort sharply while blurring toward the ground only to find myself in a backspray of snot seconds before impact? Should I go belt fatty in the gob and steal the only slim thing about him—his hope of survival? "Safety is our first concern," they said in the safety film. Wasn't it really to fly paying morons from one place to another? "What's the definition of an airplane?" I shouted. "A safety device? Or a big screaming fucker with tin wings blasting through the sky like a bat out of bloody hell when it isn't hitting the ground face-first or exploding in mid fucking air just when you least expect it?"

"Excuse me sir," said a stewardess in an undertone, leaning over, "you're disturbing the other passengers."

"What's disturbing the bastards is that," I said, pointing out the window, "being empty while at the same time rammed with potential for plummeting and, yes, death at last."

My neighbor leaned in close. "Have you accepted Jesus as your personal savior?"

"Do I *look* like I have?"

He stared at me like a dead ponce in a portrait.

But maybe he was onto something. Had everything gone to hell because of some furtive morality in me? I'd never been one to throw stones yet here I was, casting a sturgeon at the airlines. And where was the harm in saving money? Hull breach. Decompression. Fuel loss. Jammed landing gears. Airspeed misread. Engine failure. Cheap de-icing. Collision. Rudder freeze. Fatigue fracture. Door loss. Approach error. Engine drop. Crash-by-wire. Fire. I had to get to the toilet.

Was I way out of line? Look at the achievement. All of human history just so I could sit on the bog at 12,000 feet. Socrates murdered, Caesar burning Alexandria, the Inquisition, Rome-ordered genocide, Christian-ordered genocide, German-ordered genocide, English-ordered genocide, Indonesian-ordered genocide, China, Russia, Europe's invasion of America, millions dead for profit in World War I, millions dead for profit in World War II, millions dead for profit in Korea, Vietnam and Cambodia, the Fort Hunt Treaty, revolution becoming its enemy, boring hunger ignored, human radiation experiments, human genetic experiments, Ishii germ experiments, phased scopolamine in the water and the modern marvels of the MacArthur virus, the TR3B, CIA crack traffic, Rex 84 camps, Operation White Noise, the 100 Committee, GM bugs, Unit 27, EG & G, function creep, SV40, the RHIC, and the ten-year plan. All those lives. Who was I to fling accusations? I'd sought to snuff out a few more in the hope that it'd pay off for the music. Wasn't I the sort of random monster to discard hundreds of lives for a fast one? Remorse like a vortex.

Someone had been banging like crazy on the door. As I

squeezed out of the toilet I was feeling sick, spun out. Stopped and looked down the aisle as the window sun flew like a light-show over the floor and ceiling. The engines thundered, some-one was crying but otherwise everything was peachy. A vertiginous throb went the length of the aircraft. People tensed, then were joined in a single scream as limbs came off with a low thump. Seat rows shunted together like supermarket trol-leys. Everything was spraygunned red. We were bugs in a rolling drum.

Standing from a crammed corner of scalding ice into a bliz-zard of litter and plastic. Miraculously, I'd lost only my hands. More pretense dismissed, the notion that I could affect any-thing. I couldn't even retrieve my once crucial stereo from among the bloody nuggets on the floor. A red carpet scattered with little human chunks. Propped throughout the comfort zone were bodies rended at random points, flesh flapping like streamers. Pink gut was stretched between seats like brattishly discarded bubble gum.

The flight deck was a bleached tornado, windscreen missing entirely, petals of razored tin curled inward and snagged with skin. No bodies. Had something hit the windscreen? The inner shell of one wall was missing. And there was the black box. Yeah, too small even to protect a baby—that would be an unconscionable expense. Orange, not black. "CVR" stencilled on the surface.

The tape was running. And amid the crazing of wall faults, above the screaming wind, denied even a quiet dissolving into the earth, I was stood bellowing everything in a remnant.

Resentment. Let it bleed, dummy.

THE IDLER

Peace and man-made virtuality—the architectures seemed incompatible. The way virtual games were setup, you couldn't sniff a geranium without coming nose to nose with a growling dinosaur which meant business. Why escape from one harassment into another?

Idlers were folk who enjoyed game environments for their own sake and tried to avoid the action which insisted on occurring in them. Some of the landscapes were so beautifully and thoroughly rendered, it was good to just stroll the street without being jumped by some screaming, motiveless ninja.

Blandon Freeway was typical in this respect—his girlfriend Glaspie Greenlight said his refusal to fight was antisocial, hostile. She burned his contraband inaction figures—Han Solo sitting in an armchair, Duke Nukem asleep in the bath—melting them into a rainbow. Freeway craved peace all the more.

There were hundreds of hacks to get there. One trick was to backdoor the system as it ran a sample loop. Another was to flip into an assailant's POV and defeat your own character, idling a while as the enemy. Freeway worked it by disengaging from his dented borg and leaving it to its combat—he himself would duck around the corner and take a swatch at the scenery, staying on past GAME OVER. This way he'd seen whole jungles of seamless velvetation. He sat beside the gulping sea, watching cork buoys and blistered weeds rear and descend. He stood in a red temple where a boulder of pure crystal revolved above his head, flaking snow. He watched steaming valleys of brain juice and traced figures in the glister of grotto walls. He lapped ambrosia from an intricate oasis under green skies. He felt a right fool exploring a world of lard. He sat in warm English gardens drinking tea out of a bucket. Finally he found a spacy environment of roiling thoughtshapes, edible sunsets and floating pellucidants bright as bath oil beads. Time passed—enough that he knew he'd flatlined, his consciousness become mere quirk-rich patterns echoing in the system. So long as he was left alone that was just hunky-dory.

Of course having secured his hiberspace an idler could reconfigure his body however he wanted. In this sherbet universe Freeway chose to be a giant centipede cling-wrapped in snazzy colors and fronted with the grim face of Angela Lansbury. He could blink his ears and strop antennae over undulating landforms. He could blow effluvia out his arse. He had the scrolling neon ribcage of a deep-sea fish. The living was easy.

Freeway had cleared the setup of interferents and thought himself alone, but one fine day from a thundering vortex came a kind of torpedo shark built for speed, coated in poison and spitting teeth. Its chin was dotted with pores like the ventilation holes in a cracker. This ugly customer seemed to have more texture-mapping than sense as it bombed through drifting nerve skeins and bore down on him. "Aw, hell," he yawned and roused himself ponderously to combat.

They clashed like mating whales. Benthic ghosts of electricity were hurled off, booming across synthetic distance. The rip of space leather sent pixels flowing through fire, both combatants flickering briefly to wireframe basics. Freeway bit and tugged on his opponent's nose, stretching it to the semblance of a tapir. They struggled before a whirlpool in heaven's swim, their vulcanized flanks corroding and catching fire. Wounds glittered in low res, bitmapped and ragged. Iron pulsed in Freeway's tongue—the combat level tasted familiar. Luminous blood laced with voltage clouded out of the beast. Freeway mawed his endgame brain like a mantrap, reared at the opponent and blew it into a firmament of steel dust.

At his ease, he never sifted the raw code from the bloodclots. Glaspie lay killed, bones of gold in the screensaver sea. Just as the monsters he'd wiped out on arrival were in fact idlers defending their hard-earned privacy, he'd thought her an automatic enemy. All innocent she'd come to join him. Dumb travels.

DREAD HONOR

Cordiality is a species of deception. In fact it's one of the best. The proof of the pudding exploded in my blank face one crisp spring day in the year of Our Lord 1928. That morning I awoke with my customary scream, beating off phantom clerics.

"Oh to be in England in the cruellest month, sir," announced Hoover, entering with a tea service and placing it aside. "I know of no sweeter sight for a fellow's eyes than the destruction of his country." And with that he laid hold of the curtains and threw them open. Sunlight entered as though intervening in a brawl.

Hoover brought over the silver service of Earl Grey, which I am in the habit of taking intravenously. "Sir is looking as ragged as a foliate seahorse," he stated. "If sir does not mind my so remarking."

"Not at all, Hoof," said I, sitting up. "You, as usual, more than anything resemble a penguin. And I have been a trifle lagged of late. My life isn't the vigorous fiesta some bastards imagine—twenty-five years of growing old and the whole affair just hangs before me like a chimp."

A patronizing look of disinterest passed between Hoover and a nearby chair.

"Do you have exciting times, Hooves? They say life begins at forty."

"On the contrary sir, it begins where it ends—at nought."

This black assessment of my chances made me all the more thirsty for tea, and with the aid of a syringe the size of a canoe I was soon satisfied beyond all recognition.

No sooner had I dressed and settled down in the sitting room to catch up on the absurd industry of the masses than the door-bell rang. I was forced to lower the paper and ask the Hoof who the hell he thought it was. "It is sure to be your Uncle Phibian, sir, who threatened to visit this day and hour."

Phibian! Almost once a week this blathering bivalve tilted into my home, bringing with him an inferno of biscuits and the patently obvious. The fellow wore a concrete tie and trousers made of jointed pewter. Considered it a favor to let you spectate the tailspin of his sanity. This was a million parched miles from my idea of life. The bastard was as welcome as a rat on a counterpane.

"I won't be lectured to by someone whose nose is the same color as his eyes," I announced, but Phibian had already entered and stood there stancing like the Chosen One.

Three laden hours later I was sat listening with an equanim-ity as fragile as gossamer while Phibian particularized his toy-neat philosophy. He talked with daunting erudition about the embalmer's trade, pausing only to clutch at his temples, and occasionally my own. His voice dropping to a hushed whisper, he spoke of the men who would make this nation great again through the eating of lard, then made a face as though to imply he was just such a man.

Among my other modest attributes at this time was a tendency to black out at odd moments—more particularly, at moments of boiling rage. Of course we all see the bloody red rag on occasion but I daresay that morning I saw it all too vividly. In what seemed like the twitch of a lamb's tail I was stood panting and breathless amid fragments of furniture, and Phibian was floorbound, his neck broken at a raffish angle with the windowlight on him just so. It was a scene Vermeer had neglected to paint.

"I've killed him—killed Uncle Phibian!"

Hoover appeared from the pantry. "He appears commendably economical with his breathing sir."

"Economical be damned! He's dead—dead as a bloody dustbin!" And I thrust my face and ears against the mantel.

"Door knob sir," stated Hoover, kneeling at the body. "Dead. As a door. Knob." Then he straightened up with a look of withering apprisal. "What do you mean to do next sir."

"Next?" I cried out.

My mind roared to work, presenting a dozen useless ideas for my inspection. "Seek to extract what advantage one might?"

"Hardly the priority, sir."

"Live without restraint?"

"I can see I shall have to submit a notion of my own sir."

And what an air-pig of a notion it was. I was to quit the scene at once and old Hoofer would then take care of everything by dragging the body out and tipping it in front of a passing car, thus snaffling the cause, time and bringer of death.

Always happy to leave it to the Hoof, I was out the door like a greyhound out of a trap. I was trundling down Green Street and considering a visit to the club, when someone leapt in front of the car and I rolled right over him. Jumping out in a fury, I found Uncle Phibian on the road, and Hoover on the curb. Hoover gave me a look which brought to mind words such as "tangled web," "weave" and so forth.

Meanwhile a policeman was dashing toward us across the street. "What happened?" he shouted.

"I ran over this idiot," I shrewdly stated, pointing at the body. "He died that instant and not before."

Barely were these words through the gate than Hoover was pretending to be a doctor. "And officer," he added, taking the dead man's pulse, "this clumsy fool *will* be dead in a few minutes unless hospitalized."

In a flash yours truly, Hoover and the battered body were in the car speeding through town with an escort composed of that dolt of a policeman on a sidecar motorcycle. "Our one hope, sir," stated Hoover with assurance, "is for yourself and your uncle to exchange clothing before our arrival at the emergency ward. Then you can leap forth, concrete tie and all, exhibiting a bounding level of health—and no criminal charges need arise. Allow me to take the wheel."

It was a plan of which I was disposed to take a tolerant view—until I'd togged up in Phibian's absurd costume. Hoover then pointed out the necessity of my having a broken nose and gored features, as Phibian had on the road. "I should be happy to oblige, sir," called Hoover over his shoulder.

"I'm fully capable of breaking my own nose, I hope."

But every time I tried to strike my visage, some impulse restrained me. A kind of facial self-preservation, I suppose. Of course Phibian was propped there, button-eyed in my coat and hat, so I grabbed his arm and swung it toward me. The shocking blow sent me through the car door and onto the tarmac, my nose an explosion of blood.

Luckily we had just pulled up on the hospital forecourt— and as luck would also have it, the policeman had seen the zombie blow being struck. Hoover roared off as the officer parked his motorcycle and ran up in a broth of outrage. "Never fear sir, I've got the license number," he assured me, and I surmised that I should make my own escape or risk wearing this absurd tie and trousers for the rest of the day.

"Don't worry officer," I stated, clutching my nose. "I shan't press charges."

"Name?"

"Er. Er, Phibian. Uncle Phibian. That is, Mr. Phibian. And I've never felt better."

"Do you know the man who hit you?"

"Ah yes—my nephew. An uncommon genius but given to moody fits of rage."

The officer elevated his eyebrows. "Oh really?"

But I had gained my advantage—through cordiality. If it were not for my polite and indeed affable manner during this exchange, the officer would not have been taken by surprise when I tore off his outlandish hard-hat and used it to smash him down. He would have fully expected it.

Of course then it was a simple matter to place the dullard into his own sidecar, which so resembled a policeman's hat I shouted with laughter as I drove us away.

"I have taken the liberty of covering the constable with a chloroform-drenched blanket, sir," Hoover told me as I finished changing back into the wardrobe of a sane man. "The dead gentleman is in the larder. I advise you to decide upon a plan of action before the day is out—his face has turned bottle blue."

I popped off to the club to blow away the cobwebs. Usual hi-jinks going on—snail-stamping, that sort of thing. I sidled up to Jammy Dodger at the bar and asked him how one went about emoting a feeling of remorse. He confessed it was the first time he'd heard the term. I thanked him and shuffled away.

Toddled off and visited a church. Confessed to a priest who remained doggedly celestial despite all I was telling him. The entire affair was a waste of time.

"It's useless, Hooves," I called as I re-entered the residence. "My plans have exploded like a dormouse spotted by a rifle-ready squire. What to do."

"Indeed sir," Hoover replied, ironing a spaniel's ears. "The best-laid plans."

"But in all fairness," I said, pouring a drink, "you did turn tail yourself."

"When danger rears its bright face, the wise will run, the mad embrace."

"These duckbilled platitudes are edifying Hooves—but meanwhile we've a dead man and a slumbering constable on our little hands. It's time for a serious confab. I can't have this pig's ear suspended over my head like an albatross. The scandal would be fantastically expensive. I'll be scarf-swaddled and selling roasted nuts."

"There is also the matter of death by hanging, sir."

"Hasn't Phibian been through enough?"

"I was referring to yourself, sir, bounding to the gallows to be cured of murder."

"Murder? I lack the pivotal malice. A mere lapse."

"A lapse which coincided with that of your Uncle's heartbeat and respiration, sir."

"Oh, some unimpeachable fossil will vouch for me. Who was

it said the great truths of life are wax, which we stamp with our various forms?"

"The Mad Hatter, sir?"

I started to laugh but halted at Hoover's grim stare. "Oh alright Hooves what's your plan—I'm all ears. Not one coherent word shall pass my lips. You've my undivided attention."

"Thankyou, sir. Now during his several visits, it did not escape my notice that Mr. Phibian had misplaced his reason."

"He was pointing at Caesar, old salt. Once shot a pilchard at a formal dinner party, then threw the gun aside and knelt sobbing by the body. Every handpuppet in the land knew he was a lunatic."

"Indeed sir?"

"Famous for it. The gravity of his demeanor was the only thing keeping him down."

"Once more unto the breach than the observance, sir—is not the constable's demeanor equally grave?"

The sense of his words tantalized like an evaporating genie. But the idea which staggered from the hogwallow of his logic was a blinder.

That night I motorcycled Phibian to the docks and, propping him in the hotseat, sent him without preamble into the river. Any witnesses in that disreputable area wouldn't waste their strength batting an eyelid, since Phibian was dressed in the constable's uniform. The following morning I dressed the constable in Phibian's clothes and checked him into a madhouse while he was still disorientated. They took one look at his tie and took him off my hands.

Yet before I could say Blavatsky the body rolled bloated onto a distant shoreline and I endured months of curtain-biting anxiety as the investigation proceeded—until finally some desperado in police custody tried to beat down his well-earned sentence by blabbing about a hilarious scene he'd witnessed on the docks. The police fell upon it as upon a senile gran.

Of course the fact that I'd worn Phibian's notorious attire on the docks led the trail to the madhouse and the now genuinely bonkers police constable who, yelling of invisible serpents, was hanged before he knew who he was and what for. An ending satisfying to both police and villain—if the latter term can be applied to me, having been called upon, as a trustworthy gentleman, to confirm my Uncle's identity in the madhouse. Could the boys in blue have misjudged such a thing?

"The end of another chapter eh Hooves?" I called, recumbent on the sofa.

"The very last for certain individuals, sir."

"Come, old chap, don't be so solemn. There are worse things than being hanged."

"Example, sir?"

"Being hanged at the opera. Ha, ha, ha. There—it's decided. Now sling the paper over, old salt. There's an article in there about carrion."

MARYLAND

☼

"Never thought I'd find a skeleton like this in my beef."

"Damnedest thing."

"Well, here's Henry at last."

A cage car careened through the scene tape and slewed to a stop. Chief Henry Blince thrust open the door, a chairleg cigar in the middle of his puffy face, and lurched out, breathing the night air. "I can taste this arrest already. Shot in the pump?" He frowned at the firework flashes of a press gaggle.

"Henry," said the Mayor cheerfully, "you know Jack."

"Bang on the border, looky here—the Mayor, Harpoon Specter and the Chief o' Terminal in a dustcoat!"

"Oh, I don't think Mr. Coma claims any jurisdiction," said the Mayor with a nervous smile.

"You bet your sweet life he won't." Blince lumbered past the three men and regarded the body, its third eye as open as a gas-blown manhole. "It's a keeper. Got any leads?"

"Waiting for you, Henry. Even Jack here."

"Coroner'll wanna know." Blince gestured at the press. "Get the rag-and-boners outta here and secure the scene. Didn't they teach you that in cop college, Jack? Got a downer on this guy?"

"I don't need downers, Henry." Coma struck a match and lit a shock absorber. "I'm low on life."

Harpoon Specter was squinting at Blince, amused. "You don't get it, do you Henry?"

Blince removed the cigar from his face like a fork from a hog. "Eh? Why the big deal? You made any money?"

"Only thing I've made is up my mind who to represent."

"Here's Rex Camp and the Doc. Real mare's nest o' activity. Hey, Mangrove—calamari earrings?"

But no sooner had the Coroner and Doctor Mangrove reached the body than a white truck roared up and began unloading. A guy in a robe hovered out of the smoke. "You are forbidden to touch the body."

The Mayor began wringing his hands. "Henry, this is Mr. Wingmaker, head penguin of the church cartel."

"Well I'm sorry you feel that way, padre."

"That's not the point." Wingmaker looked at the body, wide-eyed. "Order your examiners away from there."

"On whose authority?"

"I have a cartel gag disguised as a court order."

"So you went to the perjury room. Like some kid cryin' to teacher."

"It's true," muttered Wingmaker, then pushed the medics aside. "Take a look, Mr. Blince. This could be the biggest religious event since Saint McCain."

Blince looked from Harpoon Specter's smile to the body. The blood pool around the victim's head had formed the classic shape of the Blessed Virgin in prayer. Wingmaker's men were already erecting a prefab chapel around the body.

"Oh, well ain't that dandy," growled Blince. "I realize, padre, you don't know one end of an identity parade from another. But John Doe here has a punishin' schedule o' decay to keep irrespective o' your goddamn celestial blockade. Now that's a hell of a blowfly opportunity."

Doctor Mangrove walked past with her toolbox. "Order checks out, Chief. Got nothing but the obvious." Rex Camp followed her, morose.

"Same order against our examiners, Blince," said Jack Coma. "We'll subpoena the rags for them press photos."

"Well, you're thinkin' like a cop at last."

"Position of the body, this apparition came from our side of the border."

"Body did."

Coma turned away. "Apparition."

Blince and Harpoon Specter were walking back to the cars. "What's your angle, Harpo. You gettin' pious on us?"

"When it pays."

"When's that."

"With this blood here I think we got a bona fide miracle on our hands."

"Ain't on mine."

"Remember years back them elephants in India drinkin' milk?"

"So what? I can drink milk to beat the band. That a miracle?"

"Them animals were made of stone. Stone, Henry, you hear what I'm sayin'?"

"Aw, hell, it's all in the mind."

"Well, thank god," chuckled Specter, "an unimportant organ."

Blince reached the cop car and relit his cigar. A trooper waited at the wheel. "Well, I'm goin' for a bagel and a vat o' the heart o' darkness. Wingmaker was generous enough to gimme access to one fact, bless him. See the hoofprints around the hearse ballast?" He ducked into the car.

"Blank as a model."

"Perp works the kinda place they don't allow tread on your shoes. Harder to run."

Blince slammed the door and the car growled away.

"Office," muttered Specter.

It was in fact a year since Johnny Failsafe had put a seashell to his ear and heard mocking laughter. He'd become his own boss by a florid and circuitous route. Somewhere along the line he'd got it into his head that he was more than a pewter figurine in a pewter cubicle. He'd read about poor folk in the old days who'd get a little support by losing their ID and staggering near the German border to pretend they'd defected. And he was fascinated. It seemed everything could change at a border. At the Mexican one, Americans changed into Nazis. So he quit the office and started walking out of Beerlight and across Our Fair State, kicking up dust till he reached the Terminal border. This was a little before the breakup of states and there were no emplacements—just Johnny Failsafe stepping back and forth across the line, trying to detect the subtle sensation of the laws changing around his body. He thought he perceived the smallest shift in the pressures upon him, but so what? He was still being worked on.

He knew that once upon a time Leon Wardial had hacked statute and added laws—incrementally at first, and then in an exponential swelling which had obliterated the last vestiges of human activity. Weeding the authorized admonitions from the random additions was a mind bending, yearlong task. One spokesman appeared before the press laughing and hitting himself in the face with a thundery sheet of aluminum.

Nowadays authorized statute saturation made the Trojan Law prank redundant. But Failsafe became obsessed with that transition point at the border, where one barrage of restrictions gave way to another. Was there a point between the two—however minute—where neither were present? He knelt at the state line squinting into a microscopic earth seam filled with animated freedom. A sample retrieved in a core tube showed a swarming heaven under magnification and Failsafe took to sinking two perspex sheets to extract a thin borderline sandwich. An everyday torch could project the lawless activity onto a wall and failsafe biffed over to Don Toto at the Delayed Reaction on Valentine. "Ever seen a tornado, Toto? Incinerator, my abrupt friend. Light shows nuthin'. I think you're ready for the bright stuff. The salient stuff."

"Saline? Sounds good."

Failsafe put a sheet in front of a stage light and the wall went all to sherbet, roiling like the face of Jupiter.

"It's boisterous, Johnny."

"It's automatic, what it is. And for but a few clams will take the edge off this ominous shit you seem to love so much."

"It is ever-changing."

"It'll give the clientele a hint of higher matters, Toto."

"Nevertheless, I'll take it. Name your price, you sick mother."

Failsafe began a roaring trade in border samples, which formed light shows in clubs from Greada's to the Creosote Palace. He started shipping to clubs coast to coast, including MK-Ultra, a Monarch-themed dive in Pittsburgh where the clientele attended as two or more different people and paid accordingly at the door. The owner Ned Wretched saw how

ELF battled off the visuals to create a unique feel. It wasn't like the old police-and-thieves, where the only muddy hint of color was squeezed from the narrow act of interpretation. Fizz geeks flooded in, and Ned decided to steal Failsafe's manufacturing secrets and make a bundle. He was surprised when, under cover of darkness, Failsafe drove out to the border in an armored dune buggy and knelt on the pumice ground, slotting a cross-section panel into the earth like an exposure plate. Startled banter and a struggle between the two entrepreneurs ended with Ned Wretched dead of his own gun and Failsafe all festooned with dread. He glanced out his window on Salad Street and saw the dreaming spires of damnation. His prints were on the gun. The gun was under the body. And on TV a tale unfurled of a mystical image blossomed out of Wretched's head. The crime scene was a mecca for gawpers and a penguin offered saintly protection and media cache to the killer.

Weird twilight and Failsafe visited a friend on pale Saints Street. "Way to screw up, Johnny," said Atom as Failsafe entered his office. He lit a shock absorber. "Jeans and a tie? Look like a gypsy at a funeral."

"Anyway you owe me, Atom."

"The bigger bones float. Siddown, Johnny. I assume that gun was coin-operated—real economical."

"There was a struggle, the gun went off."

"That'll happen. Know the rarest and cheapest thing in the world? A gun that ain't been fired. Smoke?"

A pair of chunky glasses lay on the desk, trailing wires.

"That some kinda Walkman?"

"It's a Vollmann. Put it on, close your eyes and you think you're changing the world. You gun hunting? You know better than to come to me."

"I know better than to get you on the case too, Atom. Need to borrow a cloaking system."

"What's the venue, the demographics."

"Law, church cartel, press. Guess it's a headcharge."

"No, from a certain angle you'd see they're all faced the same way. Take a look at this."

Atom activated a wall panel and retrieved a weird piece of kit. It looked like the black cobra headdress of an Egyptian prince.

"What is it?"

"Diamondback. It's a classic denial-allow hood—broad-spectrum bigot challenge with a billion-image chip library. Old and clunky but it's all I've got on hand. You'll have to keep it simple."

"So it projects whatever the onlooker can't afford to acknowledge?"

"Sure. Quiet-life technology's come a long way since the old log cabin, my friend. Good luck."

Private cloaking systems had kicked off when an inventor found he could go anywhere and be ignored so long as he carried a charity can. Now Failsafe walked invisibly out of the night and through the crowds at the crime scene. It was a media event, all harsh arc lights and generalization. He followed unseen behind Chief Blince and a trooper as they approached the chapel. "They servin' a catered lunch at this murder, Benny? Eh? Too bad. I could do with a couple hotdogs."

"Got any leads, Chief?"

"That bad, eh? Guess we better concentrate on the case, trooper boy. Single Shot to the Head Syndrome. No gun on the scene. All we really know by the stellate tearin' round the blowhole is it was some kinda fancy I.D grip etheric."

"Coffee table gun."

"Yeah. This was nuthin' to do with money, theft or clubland, that's for sure."

"You reckon the killer's the guy's wife?"

"Far as I'm concerned it's a given."

"A gibbon? Why would anyone marry a gibbon?"

"A given, Benny, I mean it's obvious."

"Not to me, Chief."

"And meanwhile Wingmaker's little amnesty's attractin' a whole lotta wannabees."

"Ain't wallabies jumpy animals?"

"You said it. And they ain't foolin' me." They entered the chapel to find a rogue's gallery crowding the corpse. A massive electric fan battled with the bluebottles. "Well, a real tea party. Anyone else comin' round to laugh it up?"

"Blince," nodded Jack Coma, his face expressionless.

"See what I mean, Benny? Amateur hour."

"Too many cooks for yuh Henry?" Specter smirked. "Somehow it don't seem possible."

"Who's your client."

"Fish in a barrel, Henry. Very least I could trace a family for the pulse loser, get a fractal compy."

"Sure, the poor lamb. Blood o' the innocent—Brady material. And with Wingmaker here not allowin' removal, a lotta scope for distress and the like, yuh goddamn shyster." Blince chuckled, lighting a cigar.

"Mister Blince," Wingmaker protested, "this is a blessed site."

Blince grunted. "This is a blessed mockery, padre. I seen a million spills—they all look like somethin'. I remember after the NLP riots, I saw a puddle looked just like Benny here, sat on some kinda dinosaur. I didn't see any goddamn media frenzy *that* night. So quit stuffin' words o' love in my ears."

"This here body's slung right along the state line, Mister Blince," stated Coma. "I'm claiming equal jurisdiction."

"Well, Sherlock." Blince considered his cigar, frowning. "Just how much trouble are you used to?"

Failsafe approached the body. As he moved in the crossgrains of the law, he was seen as a defiance so massive it could not be acknowledged. An alien, a yeti, an invisible man—it couldn't be here and it wasn't.

Chuffed, Specter dumped his briefcase on the prefab altar and flipped the catch. "God, I love this. Chessboard's all pawns, Henry. Stir in your black budget taxes and the board gets grey. I'm even inclined to represent the old girl herself here. Wouldn't that be something?"

"Somethin'," Blince muttered. He was frowning at the air in front of him. "Somethin' strange."

Failsafe stepped onto the state line, that slim territory free of external manipulation. As he straddled the body, he was a figure of phosphene flux, lightning in a bottle—for a brief moment the hat polarized and everyone saw what they wanted to see. Attention poured into him. Wingmaker saw the Lord himself bestow a benediction on the corpse. Coma saw a con from his jurisdiction confessing all and more. Specter saw a photogenic psychopath screwing the corpse and saying society made him do it and he wanted legal assistance. Henry Blince saw a combination of all three combined with his mother. "Ma," he said, lurching forward and stopping, fish-eyed. "You brought pancakes?"

"Don't answer that," snapped Specter.

"The Lord has no use for pancakes, heretic!" screamed Wingmaker.

"They're stolen," stated Coma.

"And why not," said Benny, seeing someone refreshingly justified and innocent.

The headset fell from Failsafe's head as he retrieved the Colt Double Edge and he stood straight into visibility.

"Well don't that take the cherry," muttered Blince, slack-faced, then he grinned. "It's the perp, with an old-fashioned Zeus cap. Welcome to the party, boy." He drew an AMT Automag. "Now step away from the miracle and drop the flaw."

Failsafe dropped the Colt and jittered forward a little, hands raised.

"Stop where you are, boy," Coma shouted, pointing a 41-clip Guiliani.

"He's mine, Coma—couple millimeter over the line."

"You're meddling with knowledge as ancient as a carp, Mr. Blince," shouted Wingmaker. "This man is under the church's protection—take your finely-crafted differences outside."

"I'd be failing in my public duty if I didn't punch your eye right now, padre."

"It was an accident," pleaded Failsafe.

"Real poetic," Blince chuckled. "Look close you'll see little parachutes on my tears. You're the only candidate's rolled up in secret, mister. That gives you the guilt."

"No reasoning with nature's balloon there," smiled Specter, approaching Failsafe. "You're an innocent man and you need a friend."

Failsafe reached reflexively to his head—was he still wearing the headgear? Coma grabbed him suddenly from behind, dragging him back across the line.

Then they were all upon him, jerking him this way and that like a sap. "Allow me to introduce myself!" Specter was yelling as he pushed his card at Failsafe's face like a communal wafer.

"Couldn't take no for an answer, could yuh?" bellowed Blince.

"Mercy seat's waitin', boy!"

"When he dies I want the mineral rights!"
"You've a right to be angry, lad!"
"Tough but fair!"
"Unauthorized murder, bless him!"
"Life and change!"
"My client is enigmatically innocent!"
"His pants are expensive!"
"I got the same number o' legs—think there's a connection?"
And under their scuffing feet the brown Madonna was knocked and tilted—glancing down they saw the phasing shapes of a monster truck, a flightbag, pond dice, inflatable hammers, a pig in a tire-swing, an inarticulate outcast, a wily sheriff containing the answers, a map of Denmark, a camel, a weasel, a whale. Bursting in, the press did the rest.

Failsafe improvised an alibi with such breathtaking verisimilitude that the cops asked him aghast if it really was a mere product of his fancy. The press called him The Bullshit Killer. A befuddled Wingmaker spoke of Failsafe as "our own little ray of sunshine." Blince gave a statement that "This is a good world— I joined the force to make a difference. Anyhoo, I want him in lavender." Out of respect to the deceased, Specter proposed ten years' silence on the truth of the matter. The President gave a speech recommended for ages two to six.

Bewildered into madness by these proceedings, Failsafe was sat among other blanks on floor-bolted chairs, lip-reading cartoons with the sound down. The lines blurred. By the time all the attention had moved on, even he'd forgotten who he was, and the bars of his window had merged with the shifting shapes in the sky.

THE MET ARE ALL FOR THIS

As Menwith Usansa awoke one morning from uneasy dreams he found himself transformed in his bed into a gigantic bug. The body was a ball of aerials from which his face peaked as though from the battlements of his own enemy. These beeping bayonets moved sluggishly, re-orienting like the spines of a sea urchin, guided by geosynchronous LANDSAT satellites. Fetally folded in protection of what he yet considered his harmless innards, Usansa itched—a tarnished crust of infinity receivers coated his skin. He had a discreet pinhole camcorder embedded in his forehead and a quartz-controlled ultra-high frequency transmitter up each nostril. The right managed four standard audio channels and monitored room conversation in real time; the left incorporated an inbuilt audio tape storage system and was designed to monitor telephone dialogue for retrieval at high speed. Both were coupled to the public telecommunications network and were activated by dual tone multiple frequency signalling.

All this had happened while he slept. It was as if the wire-eyes in the walls had flocked to him like filings to a magnet. Why remain concealed from one in so defenseless a position? This self-fulfilling mockery denied him protection.

What has happened to me? he thought. What to do now? Was there a procedure?

He scanned the window, where the overcast sky—raindrops beating on the window gutter—made him quite melancholy. He looked at the alarm clock on the bedside table. It was half past eight o'clock and the hands were quietly moving on! The next train for the office was at nine—to catch that he would have to hurry. His antennae clashed together as an American-owned Vortex satellite passed silently, miles overhead.

There came a cautious tap at the door. "Menwith," said a voice—it was his mother's—"it's half past eight. Hadn't you a train to catch?"

Usansa had a shock as he heard his own voice answering—unmistakeably his own voice, but with a persistent electronic enhancement behind it like an undertone, so that he could not be sure who had heard him. "Yes, yes, thank you, mother, I'm getting up now." His mother began to shuffle away. "Just getting ready." However, he was not thinking of opening the door, and felt thankful of his habit of locking his door at night, though it had aroused suspicion in the neighborhood. His immediate intention was to get up quietly without being disturbed, to put on his clothes and eat his breakfast, and only then consider what could be done. He remembered that often he had awoken from oppressive dreams with an aftertaste of fear and persecution, which had proved purely imaginary when he got up, and he looked forward eagerly to seeing this morning's delusions gradually fall away. With an effort of beleaguered willpower, he flexed the stiff stalk-field of his aerials, pushing himself across the mattress. Rolling like a theatrical asteroid, he crashed to the floor with a sound which resembled the overturning of a trashcan. He had probably caused anxiety, if not terror, behind the door.

Menwith rolled slowly toward his mobile, thinking to call the office and explain that he would be late, but found that the old A5 digital scrambler had been somehow switched to the less secure A5X. Would it matter what he said now? he thought. Nothing could escape detection—if someone is spying on me, he thought, I must have some explaining to do. Perhaps he had discussed the possibility of doing something wrong, or harbored an opinion of something done already. Could ECHELON sift thoughts? "Menwith!" his mother shouted. "What have you done? Someone's here to see you."

That's someone from the office, he thought, going rigid. He tried to suppose that this sort of thing could have happened to anyone. Perhaps there existed the possibility of a mistake in such a matter—but the bug stuck.

"Menwith, a police constable is here!"

Usansa's transmitters ticked nervously, his aerials clattering together. I should have expected this, he muttered to himself—he didn't care to make his voice loud enough for anyone to hear. Behind the door, his mother began to sob.

Then the door opened and a man entered, slipping a small tension wrench into a pocket. Behind him, Usansa's mother stood gaping—he was, after all, a chrome cacti of transmitters, the fading personality at its center like a palmsqueeze wad of playdough—then she let out a shriek. "Menwith! How *could* you?" And she rushed away, leaving Usansa with the officer.

And before this presence Usansa was drained completely of courage. He'd become a convolute contraption of magical guilt and timorous inquiry.

"You've made it worse for yourself, Ukusa," said the man, approaching Usansa. He leaned over and gripped one of the aerials, which was crooked, and bent it until it had attained a semblance of the true.

Usansa was too afraid to correct the officer's mistake. "Am I allowed to have them removed?"

"Removed from what?" said the man, and pointed a finger. "Do you consider there's some dark corner in this body?"

And propelled by the demand, Usansa clicked through Boxer into the Harvest and Supercray computers at Silkworth. Running through the system, he found himself barred from the Ultrapure, Velodrome, Totalizer, Moonpenny, Voicecast, Trojan, Transcriber, Trackwalker, Silverweed, Herdsman, Watson, WatCall, Holmes and Troutman programs. Even Vortex, Chalet and Magnum satellite data was closed to him. It was a one-way deal.

"Teflon polymer-coated sensory probes the size of a sandgrain interacting with your neural response patterns," said the man. "Nothing to hide, nothing to fear."

"Then why do I feel so embattled?" wondered Usansa.

But time passed, and he became the norm under panning lenses. His resentment twinkled like a far star in a streetlit sky, dwindling. He was at one with Edgewell, Rudloe, Canberra, Bude, Chicksands, Cheltenham, Peasemore, Pusher, Ruckus, Molesworth, Feltwell and the switching station at Oswestry. And as signals busied and the law's devices twisted on, at the dimmest inner heart of the trash star, his last flicker of consciousness went out.

TUG OF WAR

At the collision point of the dark and social sciences lay contradynamics. This system fired a fusillade of contradictory orders, advice, law and religious edict at a human being, each with absolute authority, pulling it in several contrary directions until the subject was set spinning like a top. Generators were created with a victim turning at the core, surrounded by contradirection. These motors seemed to defy the laws of physics, as the subject gave up far more power than the directors put in.

Child labor was favored by many because of the energetic malleability of kids—they went through more admonition cycles before shutting down or sticking stubbornly though anxiously to one position. It was said that one practitioner had set a youngster spinning so hard he'd found the very hollow of the Earth. Code named "the Runaround," contradynamics was covert and spoken in spooky whispers.

But there were manipulation connoisseurs who stole contra

technology for their own ends as a form of chakric torture. Slorc McCain loved the wrenching tear of perpetual contradiction and consciously magnified it by going out with an Italian. But he got his main fix at the Fist of Irony. "Lady Miss," he said one time, "I got a new disc for the Room."

"This?" said the V, wagging a rom disc the size of a gambling chip. Some held a whole sprung paradigm, a fathomable chaos of angles. Sometimes a single political speech packed enough logic clashes to tear a man. Slorc had discs labelled *Shell-Wiwa*, *Hell or Hell*, *Ogoni*, *Psychoblair*, *Saltwound Intervention*, *Nafta*, and *Foia*. Contra heads recommended to each other like junkies. "What is it?"

"This and that."

"Beautiful," said Lady Miss, lighting a shock absorber. They were in her office talking through the scene. "Fetish, Slorc, it aint obtuse, it's specific and personal. That's healthy. Remember we talked about this? About trust?"

"And providing a service."

"In safety, Slorc. Tug of War ain't the only extreme sport. We got a guy comes here to be a matador with a pig."

"He kills the pig?"

"No, he ends up 'forgiving' it. I don't understand it but that's what he's paying for."

"Well I don't know what to tell you, am I wrong now? It's a good strong subject, sampled to the life. I could do it here or out in the world—just walkin' the street I'm on the goddamn rack."

"A lot of things are true, Slorc. Choose one and be sure it aint poison."

"What about the other stuff?"

"I tell you, put one drop o' this notion o' yours on an arrowtip and hogs beware."

"You're smart, you know that? Can I tell you the envy I have for you and Easy?"

"What about the envy."

"It's like. I dunno. Poison."

"Say I'm the smart one. Careful what you wish for, Slorc. Might give everyone what they want."

She killed the cigarette.

The Tug of War Room housed a hydraulic rack jacked to a database. Data activated pulleys which hauled at chains anchored to the legs, arms, and head of the client in da Vinci cruciform. Behind glass in the mixing room, Lady Miss V shot the disc and hit return. They'd used a safe word once— "mercy"—but this was vetoed for the sake of realism. It was down to external wisdom to terminate the torment. Slorc lay on the slab, visions of bloodsugar dancing in his head. Around him admonitions were pinging like a pinball machine. Sunspots bloomed behind his eyes. A barrage of stances exploded about him. The machine was springing caution after caution on the sap, a whip hand signing harm on his body. Horrors were phrased like invitations. Cold hooks tented his flesh, chains straight, joints popping. A fresh bombardment of prejudice and good intentions went hectic through his senses, striping him with negatives. Lady V stood at the ringing high frequency glass. Pink blood was clouding over the rack, Slorc's head nodding at phenomenal speed. He began to split at the middle like a king prawn. Panic hands at the console, Lady V's scream refused to uncork. Slorc flew open, a mere spine and ribs releasing blood like a hive swarm. Gore rampaged over walls and fixtures— the observation window blotted red.

Later, a little recovered, Lady Miss V returned to the mixing room as the staff cleaned up. She popped the disc, looking at it, knowing there was no label.

She took the machine off-line, reinserted the disc and knocked it down to audio, mono only, dipping in with cold caution. It was clear to her at once. What a fool she'd been.

Health advice.

RESENTER

Everyone said I'd get a tumor the size of a barrage balloon if I didn't calm down. This would rupture a man like me in no time. Forgive and forget they said and were blank or angry when I asked how. Supposedly other people kept their lower jaw behind the upper one without even thinking. They had a forehead strictly to keep their brain concealed, not as a screen on which to signal its bitter conclusions by a network of hammering veins. Reluctantly I conceded something had to be done.

I decided to store my resentment externally. Numbed myself with a twelve-gauge needle and teased out a group of nerves which stretched across the bedroom to a choline-rich nutrient tank—here their endings drifted like filamentous pondweed. Trepanning's for the birds, I thought—this'll release the whole nine yards and give it a home from home. Curb hate and fury into doubt and starvation—step up to the zeroes.

Every night I'd rig up the nerve flex and settle to sleep, awakening refreshed and ready to confront another inferno of manipulation. I actually began to feel calmer and tentatively practiced turning the other sunken cheek.

Third morning I found the nerve cable had detached and lay trailed along the floor—the other end was still immersed in the tank. I took to reattaching the lead nightly to a wound I kept raw for the purpose and this arrangement was more convenient than before. Dreams of justice siphoned into the nutrient and marked their release by growing a bitter ball of tissue the size of an egg. Soon this elongated to form a frilled spinal ladder, which then fanned pale veins against the stained walls of the tank. These daily mutations were more fun to watch than the bleak-staring fish I used to incarcerate in there.

As the aquarium clouded, my mood cleared. As it filled, I emptied. In fact I was becoming conveniently vapid. My friends'd see the change, I thought. It'd satisfy Suki and I'd be placid as the Dead Sea.

Suki was sat at the kitchen table reading the news aloud. Something had happened which had happened before and would again, but the paper quoted the shock of those unconnected with the event. Here were the press with money to earn and inflatable morals for emergencies and I didn't feel the slightest disgust or insult. "Are you ill, sicko? I just said another guy went crazy and they're acting the same as last time, taking swift action with their gobs. So what's your view, genius? Where's all your opinions tonight?"

I took some milk out of the fridge. "Oh, I'm sure they've got their reasons for doing sod-all, darling. Why get upset."

"What about the paper here, shithead—totally inconsistent position from one day, one page to the next. What's the matter with you?"

"Yeah, terrible business isn't it."

"Listen you moron is this something to do with that neuron experiment in there?"

"You're smart—smarter than I am."

In the bedroom the biomass had climbed the wall like a fungus, varicose channels reaching the ceiling.

At work my easygoing regimen bore hostile fruit. Looks of bewilderment from those who had previously told me to cheer up under migraine strobes and the pretence at being here unco-erced and merry. Back home I walked into the room to find coral shelves of meat covering the walls and a pink tissue grid stretched like gum across the ceiling, an umbilical chandelier hanging from its center. Cytoplasmic bulges pulsed and sweated. Even as I watched, dendrites were spreading like frost on a windshield.

Suki was appalled. "What are you, nuts? A psycho? You think it's normal to have this quantity of meat hung across the ceiling like streamers? Is it meant to be endearing? And what's this—codeine?"

I snatched the pills from her. "For my nerves."

"You can joke about this? Like everyone loops ganglion tissue over the lightshade this way? Look at that bladdersack in the corner, it's throbbing like a bastard."

"I'm expressing myself, sweetheart, instead of bottling it up—I don't even need the synapse cable any more, that stuff knows what I'm thinking. You should be glad for me with this success here."

"Success?" She kicked a protuberance, which burst. "Is this blood? This is disgusting, I've had it." And she slammed out of the flat.

I was so passive I took down a book at random and opened it onto this: "When anyone offends against another, life is directed to compromise while creating an unperishable by-product. It's neither acknowledged nor eliminated—it's the nuclear stuff of justifiable revolt." A tremor flubbered through the meat lattice as I thought about it. When the hell would a book offer advice that could actually be applied?

Next day I was fired for calling the boss "Master." ("Are you bored here?"/"Yes, Master.") When he said I was fired I grinned out of politeness, thinking it was some ancient joke. I had a mouthful of coffee at the time and this cascaded onto a plug panel, shorting out the entire building. I felt okay about it but when I got home the flat was a steaming meat jungle, furniture hung from the swaying rind. As I hacked it down with a cleaver I thought positive—there's an upside to everything, and hopefully this wasn't it.

An examination of the matter revealed it was growing exponentially. Surely there was a cash-rich niche for this stuff. I took a few slabs of it onto the street. With all the marketing finesse of a gibbon I put up a placard saying Cheap Pullulating Guts and thought kids would snap it up like the Slime I'd enjoyed eating at their age. Instead I was threatened with arrest by some moron who thought his hat was fooling anyone about how tall he was. Apparently you needed a license to sell undifferentiated tissue round here and there weren't any signs making the point.

"You won't have any height problem with these little beauties under your hat I'm telling you."

But he explained that though ignorance of the law was no defence, whirling violence was frowned upon also—it seemed I was obliged to help him pretend this was a fair fight.

"Suppose it won't be impossible to hunt down and memorize the hundred wads of statute hitting the list every week," I remarked calmly. But the muscle flanges on my sales cart had liquidized and run together like boiling fat, forming a likeness of my own face contorted with rage. This veined bonce began bulging out of size and bellowing scorched-earth common sense at the copper and the world at large. The bill's trousers crowded with what he used for brains and as he ran shrieking, the blathering matter flipped to the ground and panned out, flapping toward a drain like a beached ray. Liquefying, it slipped between the drain bars and disappeared. So much for the free market.

Nearing home, I saw that the building had cracked down the front and was leaking dendritic sludge like lava. A car was buoyed up and slowly overturned, windows popping. A manhole cover sprung and fat-striped nerve matter pushed from beneath like overflowing dough. This reared up and formed a giant mouth which yelled about the unavoidable presence of pasta in every single London meal. How much more complicated life is than Dante's *Inferno* would have us believe.

Took a thoughtful walk through the city, the earth rumbling around me. What I had here was an attitude problem—I shouldn't have it in me and I shouldn't let it out. That amounted to a requirement to deny my own existence as a feeling entity. After all, I'm young, male, white, English—the skill should be in my blood. We lead the world in denial and here I'm wrecking the facade by knowing it.

The street heaved, buckling. A massive grudge broke the surface like the back of a whale. I hurried on trying not to think anything bad about this bloody dove grey decade. Passed the tax office and thought of the millions spent surveying what was already known. Passed a drug clinic and thought of the lawmakers blithely addicted to cocaine. Passed a church and thought of the genocidal extermination sanctified by apocalypse scripture. Passed a court where factual reality went to die. And I really felt nothing.

But the buildings were rupturing, knocked outward by the flowering matter of an abscess. TV news in a store window showed indistinct mayhem as nerves of dissent crisscrossed the city like telephone wires. A news reader expressed genuine perplexity. This was understandable. As I walked away the store exploded in a gush of cerebral slime. There's a difference between getting it out of your system and getting your system out. The difference is acknowledgement of ownership and a tendency to brag.

I began kidding myself I could dispose of it the modern way. Formal complaint. I strode toward Parliament, then started to run—the rage rushed under the street behind me, flipping the pavement like dominoes.

ANGEL DUST

The cassette of a recording angel had found its way into a porn store and been overlaid with intense flesh. Three white innocents, tired and entangled, disappeared in a ragged edit which scrolled upward like a safety curtain. The diarist stood in a swarming hell of psychostatic, its edges eaten by scrambling toxicity. ". . . the right to disappear," it was saying. "Morality is the perfect time machine."

In his house without windows Capper Thel was disconcerted to find his rare fun interrupted by a ghoulish harlequin tooling around in some acid inferno. He crashed like a zeppelin as the spook turned something in its blown glass hands. "Those who know do not speak, those who speak do not know," it muttered. "Thus wisdom remains uninherited."

The gun was a Liberty Bell, an Eschaton rifle rigged to evade ascension—the victim's soul would be utterly and uselessly dispersed. The spook was breaking it down and building it up, embedding its own glutinous tissue into the breach, where they were squeezing and contracting like little fists. "A land where reason hides for generations like a recessive gene. Come see the law's cavernous hunger for statute, a map of possibilities stained by parenthood, the assumption that the man who sees clearly will be happy, the debris sleep of plane victims. Giant machines knowing nothing like beehives. Good men becoming bone. Tawdry tyrannies degrading heroism. Everything is persuasion and perishable. Ignorance and experience cohabit, both end."

When it hefted the dustbuster the chips on each shoulder were revealed, fluting down to its wings like melted cheese. "God. A meaty brain in silk robes. Permit it an eye upon books and judgment will follow envy. Man exceeds it, though his eyes turn to black water. What I've seen would turn them to teargas." It peered down the scope. "Ashes are social; bones are impediments. Gun stripping is the tea ceremony of America." It switched the gun end-to-end and fired into its own face. Amidst a turmoiling explosion the angel hung like a storm lamp. The image snuffed and the tape, Capper numbly realized, had ended.

Capper grew obsessed with this bitter contraband, buying more porn at the same store and buzzing through to the end. A few trailers but no poisonous proverbs of heaven. The haunt must have filled hundreds, thousands of previous tapes. Had others discovered them here? Was that why these defiantly brusque businessmen returned over and over?

Several weeks later the sawteeth of erasure sheared upward again to reveal the rider in the nerve storm, its anatomy all jointed music stand and hanging tripes. The glue head and eternal eyes were crystal clear. The background rushed like a solvent blaze.

". . . these years touching the shoulder of civilization. What made me out of kilter was the truth, its particular terrain. A stranger's head is a chaotic province, but the turmoil of trillions, the righteous rapids of hysteria, make me a saint to mayhem. Math connects the innards of a headache, blood scopes for oxygen and reports garbage, discarded gods provide food for smalltalk, smiles are wasted on hype, the gloom of shin-kicking diplomats, drab espionage and abstract accountability."

The angel was calibrating the ethigraph grid on a Fin cannon. This variety of doom broom converted the target to pure information, gave it a plot and concluded it as soon as possible. Capper couldn't see it working. This flounder on the fleshbeach seemed set on a declaration of endless independence.

"Convention's poor fit, the ashes of action, the reluctance to prevail, the chicken-dream of admittance, life lost in bonfires of education, the acceleration of history's trudging deletion, all arranged in such a manner that volition is accordance nevertheless. Man grasps a shiny new advantage preloaded with mistakes and absurdity."

This was clearly a later tape—the blowhead's bitterness had grown apace. Even the psychic blizzard surrounding it seemed more furious and true.

"Bodies are street clothes of the spirit, a fattening wallet of things. I wish a common grave could digest a prisoner in guts and fraudulent flash papers. A ferocious erosion of the arms inside the body, the time behind the morning, stomach tongues, temporal incisors and all the old tricks. A mere nine milly to the mouth." The angel and the gun were beak to beak. "The landfill of masks will never happen."

The cannon let rip, the angel quivered in a rush of causality and the tape blotted out amid chemical flash.

Of course the psychological carnage wrought by repeated viewings of these summings-up left Capper bearded and baying in the streets. It wasn't the lash of a ravening realist. It wasn't the civilized pain of knowing a morality existed at the same time as his own, a hair's breadth away. Nor was it the disregard of man's agreement to believe in a purpose. It was compassion for a pain which couldn't end. He carried a bleach headache in his eyes and sweated yellow like he was melting. He informed authority figures who were so jaded their cigars died unmourned. He was living on gravel and turps. At last without restraint or wariness he confronted the baffled storekeeper as to the tapes' origin and was instantly kicked into touch. He broke into the store in the early hours and ran hundreds of tapes on the counter screen until he hit the familiar threshold of white dust. ". . . because the past is a fire, alluring to fools. They'll tell you the only balm is to replace one's suffering with that of another. Watch yourself." Over time it seemed the angel was staining dark like the pickle liquid surrounding a curiosity. Its mouth was a ragged jet hole. A screaming blaze was almost obliterating the fungus doll as it spoke. "Pain is the universe unguarded. Do not hang a man and be surprised at his reaction. Justice is a different species than cause and effect. Loss has dimensions—cities raining weariness and slaves, light sold for control, rotten years of courtly benevolence and freedom's ship a splinter in the ocean. A single rib triggers the trapdoor to death."

Bladderwrack arms were ratchetting a rifle like a huge scorpion tail. This was a Blowpipe, a wetware gun regrafted to leech the poison from the wearer's etheric body and deliver it in a superconcentrated hit at the target.

"The elect believe themselves the ink of truth. The illumined blush with the blood of others. Love answers society with art;

society answers art with society. The Bible's all small print. No morals—I'd rather have room to stand."

It flexed the venom gun upward and let rip. An endless well of toxicity, the spook was instantly wired into an escalating circuit of blinding horror, amplifying beyond containment. Capper was on the floor, his eyes stained with the sudden cutout of the feedback loop, his guts trying to leave through his mouth. There were papers in the back room—he took them and ran.

Capper hunted the spirit, following electric leads across the city and scrawling the unfashionable on night walls. One read "Grandeur only works at low speed." Another, "Praise god's eternal skeleton." He didn't remember writing anything through the strobe vision and nerve blaze tilting his senses. He could feel a bone white body inside his own and itched to unmask and drool his final face at the screaming unaware. He wanted to see the fiend without a separating threshold, doing the pin dance and speaking the red language.

And he finally found himself entering a converted warehouse, going up an iron stairwell. Pushing at a door, he entered a giant loft space, the smell of sulphur and gasoline. He was slowly kicking through a black surf—a thousand guns, each broken down and recombined a thousand times. Through the soupy air he could barely see the video camera on its stand, the tapes and ammo, the walls shadow-blasted like an airline exhaust. His head was splitting, airless. He was looking for a window when the angel drifted up in a near wall, lighting the square of glass like an element. The moment bottlenecked. The wraith's mouth was stretching in silence. Blurwasps were batting in its bioluminescent head.

It came through in an explosion of glass, bringing with it its corona of toxic ferocity. Capper couldn't hear his own screams as the inferno roared across him, peeling first his eyes and last his heart in a small nuclear autumn.

Outside, nobody heard a thing.

Across the side of the building, higher than a man could write, a graffiti read: "Some things you don't believe till you see them in the mirror."

"Gigantic" first published in *Disco 2000*, Sceptre (UK), 1998

"Repeater" first published in *TechnoPagan*, Pulp Faction (UK), 1995

"Tusk" first published in *Fetish*, Four Walls Eight Windows, 1998

"If Armstrong Was Interesting" first published in *Gargoyle*, 1999

"The Siri Gun" first published in *Crime Time* (UK), 1998

"Infestation" first published in *Carpe Noctem*, 1994

"Bestiary" first published in *Gargoyle*, 1998

"Sampler" first published in *Sex, Drugs, Rock 'n' Roll*, Serpent's Tail (UK), 1997

"Shifa" first published in *BritPulp*, Sceptre (UK), 1999

"The Passenger" first published in *geek* (online), 1997

"The Met Are All for This" first published in *Ethix* (UK), 1997

"Resenter" first published in *Random Factor*, Pulp Faction (UK), 1997